THE QUINTESSENCE OF AUGUST

Borgo Press Fiction by BRIAN STABLEFORD

THE QUINTESSENCE OF AUGUST

A ROMANCE OF POSSESSION

BRIAN STABLEFORD

THE BORGO PRESS

MMXI

THE QUINTESSENCE OF AUGUST

Published by Wildside Press LLC

www.wildsidebooks.com

DEDICATION

For Barbara

CONTENTS

AUTHOR'S NOTE

This short novel is the fourth story in a sequence; although the story is independent and self-contained, some reference is inevitably made to the earlier elements of the series. "The Legacy of Erich Zann" can be found in a Perilous Press volume in company with a short novel from outside the series *The Womb of Time*, while *Valdemar's Daughter* and *The Mad Trist* make up the two halves of Wildside Double #10.

In addition to the nineteenth-century sources of inspiration that are intrinsic to the series, this story draws significantly and crucially on ideas contained in a paper by Isabella van Elferen, "Music of Other Spheres: Diagonal Time and Metaphysics in *Lost*," which I first encountered when I heard it read at the founding conference of the Gessellschaft für Fantastikforschung in Hamburg in October 2010. I am grateful to Dr. Van Elferen for letting me see the fuller version of her essay, published in *Science Fiction Film and Television*, Vol. 3 No. 2 (2010), pp. 253-270, and for allowing me to plunder various notions and phrases that I have adapted, in an admittedly cavalier fashion, to the purposes of the story.

"How much finer things are in composition than alone."

Ralph Waldo Emerson, Journals (1833)

"Who is there that, in logical words, can express the effect music has on us? A kind of inarticulate unfathomable speech, which leads us to the edge of the Infinite, and lets us for moments gaze into that!"

Thomas Carlyle, On Heroes,
Hero-Worship and the Heroic in History (1841)

"'Then the Egregore....'

"'Attaches itself to its own sex, in contrast to the ghoul, incubus or vampire. Their malevolent work is self-explanatory; it is with their kisses, with the accursed fire of their knowing caresses that they melt the flesh and the health of the living like wax. Their bedchamber is the Devil's crucible. The incubus drains and kills his mistress with sensuality; the succubus breathes in and drinks the wine of her lover. They are sent down here one after the other as accessories to the attraction of the sexes and the everpresence of lust. The Egregore is another thing altogether. It is the unfeeling and deleterious influence of a creature of darkness, of a dead man or a dead woman which instals itself beside you in the guise of a living one, insinuating itself into your life, your habits and your admirations, meddling with your heart and taking odious root there, while its damnable mouth breathes a fatal passion into you: a commonplace madness; the folly of the artist or the amateur. And step by step, it increases the delusional and fascinating obsession, until you lie down one fine evening in the cold of the grave....'"

Jean Lorrain, "The Egregore" (1888)

CHAPTER ONE
AUGUST IN PARIS

Monsieur le Chevalier Auguste Dupin was not the kind of man to follow convention, and he sometimes gave the impression of being immune to the ordinary discomforts to which human beings are routinely subject—or, if not immune, at least oblivious. No matter how hot, odorous and vermin-infested Paris became in the month of August, he never imitated his fellow citizens by retiring to the country, either to the increasingly popular resorts of Normany and Brittany or to the bracing air of the mountains of the Massif Central and the Alps. Perhaps he felt that his forename gave him some kind of strange and special kinship with the month, although he was not normally the kind of man to turn wordplay into private superstition. At any rate, the year of 1846 was no different in that respect from its ten predecessors, and presumably many more that I had not been present to count.

It might have been the case, of course, that Dupin simply considered that he did not have the financial means to transplant himself in the conventional manner, and it was therefore out of the question. Throughout the time I had known him he had never had any obvious source of income, and was often without a sou in his pocket, although I had always assumed that he was a *rentier* of sorts and that his frequent lack of ready funds had more to do with absent-mindedness than absolute poverty. He certainly seemed to be able to fund his prodigious appetite for esoteric books, and I never heard any of the book-dealers with whom he had dealings on a regular basis complain that he was slow in settling his account. In other ways, his lifestyle was conspicuously modest, but by no means lacking in respectability; although he had been glad to lodge with me for a while, until the mild pressure of my incessant company had proved to much for him, he had continued to pay the rent on his apartment in the Rue Dunôt. He cannot possibly have treated the latter building's concierge in a miserly fashion, for the fearsome old gorgon manifested a fervent loyalty to his instructions and interests.

Having a more than adequate income myself, I would, of course, have been glad to pay his expenses had he condescended to take a holiday in the deadliest month—for some unaccountable reason of petty psychology I would have found that less irritating than the fact that he was hardly ever able to settle the fare for a cab he had ordered—but he always refused any such offer, even on occasions when I insisted on going to the Breton coast regardless, and assured him how much more I would appreciate the holiday were he to come with me. The only effect of such pleading was that I felt guilty if I left him behind. More than once, therefore—and 1846 was one of those years—I steeled myself to endure the inferno that Paris became in August, and remained in the capital.

August is, of course, an anomalous month in the city, not so much an intrinsic part of the calendar as an acknowledged gap therein. In rural communities, August is harvest time, the climax of the agricultural year: a time of sustained labor, whose generous warmth serves to generate pride, satisfaction and joy; but in great cities, where there is no harvest, but merely a vacuum of demand that will ultimately soak up every vestige of the surplus of the land, the mean heat takes on very different connotations, becoming an agent of dehydration, suffocation and hallucination. For centuries, cities have been partially depopulated in August, as large numbers of humble folk who have come in search of work or education return to their family homes in order to help gather in the harvest, while the aristocrats who have traditionally maintained two homes leave their town houses empty and take up residence in their châteaux. In cities, August is a month for flight, for escape, for taking refuge—and for those left behind, earthbound, imprisoned and exposed, it can be a dispiriting and dangerous time.

In cities, August heat-waves kill, and that is nowhere more true than in Paris. August is August throughout the northern hemisphere, in Boston, London and Naples as well as Paris, and in all of those other cities toxic heat-waves increase discomfort, delirium and mortality, among those who stay behind. In Paris, however, the effects always seem exaggerated to an unusual degree, perhaps because Paris is the most delirious city in the world even in the soberest of months. It is also the one that has drawn the greatest contrast between its own fetid enclosure and the vast sprawl of its surrounding provinces—provinces that it considers to be its dependencies, although, as a huddled city, it is entirely dependent on them for its material nourishment, if not its food for thought and imagination. It is perhaps unfortunate that imagination thrives on fetor and enclosure, while thought does not: a circumstance that readily gives rise to hauntings and demonic afflictions.

Winter is sometimes considered to be the optimum time of year for hauntings and diabolical mischief, by virtue of its long hours of darkness, but larvae are by nature *frileuse*—they feel the cold excessively, by virtue of being chilly themselves—and the residents of Pandemonium find earthly heat pleasantly mild by comparison with infernal fire. All entities of those ambiguous kinds would naturally prefer August to January, especially in cities, and most especially of all in Paris. (Let it be understood, in case there should be any confusion, that I am speaking poetically. As a rational man, I do not quite believe in larvae or demons. Even the most rational of men, however, is only a little more than a bundle of doubts, fears, anxieties and apprehensions, and I cannot bring myself entirely to disbelieve in such things either. I have, as Dupin would put it, an open mind. In August, when I stay in Paris, it is more open than at any other time of the year.)

To speak in terms that are no less poetic, but not so heavily loaded with mere superstition, it has always seemed to me that in big cities during August—even in the Boston of my childhood, let alone the Paris of my maturity—the Classical elements of which the mundane world is supposedly composed are not only thrown out of balance by a surfeit of fire and earth and a dearth of air and water, but slyly supplemented by a fifth: not the pure celestial aether which the ancients credited to the world outside their capsule Earth, but a very different quintessence, metropolitan rather than celestial and more purulent than pure.

Or, to put it in terms that are not poetic at all, my constitution is such that I am ever vulnerable to sunstroke, and hence to exhaustion, hallucination and distress—but my great friend Auguste Dupin never left Paris in August, and there were many years in which I allowed him, perhaps unwisely, to serve as my anchor. In that respect, 1846 was not unduly exceptional.

Oddly enough, and perhaps paradoxically, Paris in August never seems much less crowded for its conventional depopulation. That is partly because its transient population expands to compensate for the decline in its permanent population. In 1846, as in other years, a substantial fraction of those who had left the city to help with the harvest also helped bring the glorious abundance of the harvest back to Paris, for the purposes of boastful exposition as well as mere trade; they came home in the early morning, even if they were gone again long before noon.

Then again, while the inhabitants of Paris went on holiday to kinder climes, tourists took advantage of their own calendar-determined vacations to visit Paris—especially Englishmen, who are rumored to share a fearlessness of sunstroke with mad dogs. 1846 was not a good year for English tourists, however; although still two years short of the so-called Year of Revolutions, it was nevertheless a time of ferment and anxiety. The politics of Louis-Philippe's reign were not far removed from desperation, and although the marriage of his youngest son to the princess of Spain was still two months away in August, relations with England were already deteriorating markedly.

Exotic creature that he was, Dupin never seemed to suffer from heatstroke, dehydration or the general somnolence that seemed to settle upon the left bank like a blanket when August hit its stride. As for the stink from the Seine—well, even I became accustomed to that in time, and if we ever mentioned it to one another at all, it was only to compare it favorably with the reek of the Thames, the pestilence of the Tiber or the degradation of the Nile.

As a self-declared connoisseur of darkness—in the spirit of deliberate perversity that he cultivated, so as to keep his mind free of insidiously seductive preconceptions—Dupin did not entirely approve of the lingering daylight that lit the capital long into the evening in June and July, and found in the fact that the evenings drew in somewhat during August a measure of compensation for the stifling heat. Indeed, the late evening became his favorite time of day in August, when the temperature dropped to a near-tolerable level and the dark atmosphere seemed to acquire a kind of silkiness that it never possessed at any other time of year. He often condescended to spend five or six evenings a week in my company, sitting outside one of the *bistros* or *cabarets* in the vicinity of Saint-Germain-des-Prés, sipping a cognac or a *petit mominette* and discussing developments in science, philosophy, literature, or even music.

I say "even music" because Dupin's attitude to music was a trifle odd; he had what might be termed a *passionate theoretical* interest in it—if that combination of terms is not oxymoronic—but never went to concerts or played an instrument. My own interest was much more immediate; although I found the routines of Parisian social intercourse as difficult and taxing as my friend, I did love to attend recitals and musical plays of every sort. My memory is not perfect, and I cannot remember now all the things we discussed on the evening when the story that I am about to relate reached out to bear us away in its narrative flow, but I am perfectly certain that the music of Frédéric Chopin—by which I was particularly enthused at the time, all the more so because the great man's health was said to be failing—must have been one of them. I do remember becoming slightly annoyed on more than one occasion when I tried to describe the quality of that great composer's work—especially his nocturnes—to Dupin, who was intensely interested, but had never actually heard Chopin play. It seemed to me, when I made my ineffectual attempts at description, that the exercise was slightly ludicrous, given that he could have learned so much more simply by accompanying me to an actual performance.

"If you were not the most scrupulously rational man in the world," I said to him, once—perhaps on the evening when the adventure began, although I cannot be sure—"I would suspect your attitude to music of being frankly superstitious. It is almost as if you had some kind of covert fear of exposing yourself to it excessively. Whenever there is a singer or a violinist performing in one of the *cabarets* in which we drink, you always seem to be wary of sitting too close, and sometimes appear to be deliberately ignoring the performance."

"Do I?" he queried. "I appreciate your bringing it to my attention, because it is not something of which I am consciously aware—although I readily accept that it might be true."

"I have noticed that you seem to have a particular aversion to the gypsy violinists who abound in the capital in the late summer," I told him, "especially when they begin to play tunes of a plaintive nature, as they tend to do when dusk falls in a gentle fashion and day turns gradually to night."

"I commend you on your improving powers of observation," he said, in a tone that was a little less than wholly appreciative.

"You're not the only one who shrinks away from performers of that sort, mind," I said, hoping to ameliorate the insult, "especially when they run their fingers along the strings to make a sound like the screech of a dying cat—supposedly symbolic, I assume, of the extinction of honest blue daylight in the bloody chaos of sunset."

"Very poetic," he said, dryly. "I assume that you are referring to the effect known as *glissando*, or, more rarely, as *porta-*

mento."

"Quite probably," I conceded. I saw such Italian terms routinely on concert programs, but had somehow never managed to get the hang of them.

"That might explain my reflexive aversion," he said. "*Glissando* and *portamento* are inherently transgressive movements from one pitch to another, and even though they must perforce conclude when the violinist's sliding fingers come to a stop, they point the way toward infinity. Because music has an intrinsic relationship with time, and with being, *glissando* inevitably symbolizes transgressions in time and being, often pointing a warning finger toward those kinds of infinity we call chaos and oblivion. My instinctive reaction only serves to demonstrate my sensitivity to such issues."

"Maybe so," I conceded. "Has your excessive sensitivity anything to do with that wretched book you have on your shelves? The one that's the envy of every bibliomaniac and occultist in Paris, to an extent that makes me wonder why no one has stolen it from you during the last dozen years?"

"Which book is that?" he countered, with blatant disingenuity.

"Don't tease me, Dupin—you know very well what book I mean. *Les Harmonies de l'enfer*, by the self-styled Abbé Appolonius."

"Oh, *that* book," he said, with a slight sigh. "Sometimes, I could almost wish that one of the many lunatics avid to possess it *had* stolen it, in order to relieve me of the impossible and vexatious task of trying to determine exactly where and how extensive the fugitive truth lurking within in it might be…but I could not bear the thought, however slim the possibility might be, that someone else might triumph where I have so far…well, if not entirely failed, have certainly not fully succeeded."

"Perhaps you might be better equipped to succeed," I suggested, "if you actually listened to more music—and not just café music, but works of innovative genius played in concert halls. We are privileged to live in such a rich era, musically speaking: Chopin, Berlioz, Schumann and Liszt, to name but a few, have added vastly to the catalogue of great works within the last decade—and if music celebrating the transition from light to darkness, or pointing the way to infinity, affects you so profoundly, you really ought to acquaint yourself with Chopin's *nocturnes*, which are infinitely sweeter and more reassuring than the incessant menacing screech of gypsy music."

He actually frowned, as if it were a bad thing that there were so many innovators of genius active in the capital of Europe. I assumed that he could not be disapproving of the fact that *nocturnes* had become so fashionable, since he was such a lover of the night himself. "You're probably right," he conceded, in the irritating fashion he had of agreeing in such a way as to make agreement sound like contradiction. "Perhaps I am too restricted in my intellectual methods, too careful in my procedures, but…."

I never found out what the "but" in question was. For a pedant, he was sometimes strangely reluctant to finish his sentences.

For the sake of the aesthetic neatness of my narrative, it would probably be better if he had been interrupted in the middle of some crucial and philosophically significant sentence by the arrival of the self-styled Comte de Saint-Germain on the evening on which the adventure began, but I can remember quite clearly that he was not. Even if our conversation about gypsy music, *glissando* and nocturnes had taken place earlier on the night when the adventure began—my vague memory of which is far more likely to be a trick of organizing consciousness than a mere recollection—I can remember with perfect clarity that no abrupt interruption was involved when the charlatan made his entrance.

Our chatter on the fateful evening had, in fact, lapsed into one of those contented silences that did not seem to trouble us as much as more assiduous conversationalists. Neither of us was in the least weary, despite the lateness of the hour, but we had drifted off into separate reveries while the dregs of our last cognac were reduced to mere stains in our glasses. We both

started in surprise when the newcomer suddenly and unceremoniously slammed down a third chair at our table, and then
sat upon it heavily, with the attitude of a man acting under an
unpleasant obligation.

"Don't go, gentlemen," was the first thing he said—although
neither of us had made the slightest twitch that might have signified a desire to run away. "I need to talk to you."

I had not seen Saint-Germain since May, when he had given
me a copy of *The Mad Trist* while I was on my way to the
Messageries, asking me to pass it on to Dupin. I still had not
the slightest idea what his true intentions had been in giving me
the book—whether he sincerely believed that it carried a curse
that would afflict one or both of us, or whether it really had been
a gesture of simple generosity, made in the interest of making
peace between us—but I felt entitled to be wary of the man in
either case. The intervening months had not been uneventful,
though, so I had hardly given the affair of the book a second
thought since my return to Paris, and there was no anger or
fierce suspicion in my wariness.

Dupin, of course, did not like the recently-elected President
of the Harmonic Philosophical Society of Paris at all, and I was
not surprised when he greeted the poseur's appearance with a
stare of which a basilisk might have been envious, while main-
taining perfect silence.

Saint-Germain met the stare frankly, and seemed inclined,
at least momentarily, to combat silence with silence. When the
silence became uncomfortable, I was the one who broke it.

"What do you want with us, Saint-Germain?" I asked, feeling
not the slightest guilt about the surliness of my tone or the omission of his fake title.

Saint-Germain did not spare me a glance, continuing to meet
Dupin's stare. "I need your help, Monsieur Dupin," he said, as
if he were spitting out a mouthful of acid that he had mistak-
enly gulped. It was obvious that it cost him dear to say such a
thing—which suggested that it really did seem to him to be a
case of dire necessity.

Dupin was in no hurry to reply, so I stepped into the breach again. "Why on earth should *we* help *you*?" I asked.

This time he did look at me, and his gaze made it clear that that there was no *we* involved, so far as his plea was concerned, although what he actually said was infinitely more diplomatic.

"Why shouldn't you?" he asked, in a far less acidic tone. "I've never done any harm to *you* at all, and I've done my level best to make up for any slight injury I might have caused to Monsieur Dupin. I helped him out in February—a gesture that has cost me dear, I might add, since Jana Valdemar found out that I was the one who set up the lanterns for the little masquerade—and I made him a present of a very valuable book in May." He turned back to Dupin then, and continued: "I don't claim to be a good man, by your exacting standards, but I don't admit to being the double-dyed villain that you seem to consider me to be. In any case, I'm not here with any malicious or treacherous intent; I'm asking for your help, because I need it, and it would be churlish of you to refuse it…even though I cannot guarantee that it would be entirely safe for you to offer it."

That suggestion was far more likely to have the effect of a lure than a deterrent, and I am sure that Saint-Germain knew it.

"What kind of help do you need, Comte?" asked Dupin, in his mildest and mot scrupulous tone.

"Someone is trying to do me harm," Saint-Germain replied. "I need to discover who it is—and, perhaps more importantly, why."

Again, Saint-Germain was well aware that Dupin loved a puzzle, the more complex and convoluted the better.

"You could go to the Prefecture," Dupin pointed out.

"Yes, I could," Saint-Germain replied. "And they would fob me off, partly because they don't approve of me any more than you do, and partly because they really are stretched beyond their limits in terms of their resources and their methods. Besides which, in coming to you I *am* recruiting the services of the Prefecture, am I not? If rumor is to be trusted, you have the ear of Monsieur Groix himself whenever you care to whisper into it—and even if that suggestion is exaggerated, you are certainly very popular in the Rue de Jérusalem, where your reputation for omnipotence and omnibenevolence is exceeded only by God's."

Dupin's answer was interrupted by the arrival of a weary waiter, belatedly responding to Saint-Germain's arrival. "Bring us a bottle of Armagnac," Saint-Germain said, off-handedly, "and three clean glasses." It was not clear whether he was talking to the waiter, to us not to himself when he added, in a tone not much above a murmur: "We might be here for some time."

CHAPTER TWO
SAINT-GERMAIN'S STORY

"If you think that you can obtain our cooperation by getting us drunk...," I began—but I stopped when Dupin made a censorious gesture.

"What makes you think that someone is trying to harm you, Monsieur de Saint-Germain?" Dupin asked, when the waiter had gone back inside to fetch the brandy.

"I don't want to make the story any longer than it has to be," the fake Comte replied, "but I need to tell you that I once spent some years in Venice, where I happened to make the acquaintance of a certain family of *bravi*—who, for reasons I need not specify, incurred a small debt to me. As you must know, the *bravi* are men of honor, in spite of sometimes becoming involved in...unsavory activities...and as you also know, they sometimes find it politic to flee their homeland. When they do, they often end up in Paris, which is something of a home-from-home for Italian...." This time, he had to grope for an appropriate word, obviously not wanting to use any of those that sprang to my mind, which included "criminals", "bandits" and "assassins." In the end, he settled on "refugees"—and then paused, as if to judge Dupin's reaction. Dupin did not bother to correct him.

"Well," said Saint-Germain, "it so happens that one such refugee had acquired something of a reputation as a reliable hireling in matters lying beyond the scope of the law. He was approached with a view to acquiring his services, but when he found that the designated victim of his attentions was me, he felt obliged to refuse the commission. Indeed, he felt obliged to come to me and warn me that someone was trying to hire an agent to obtain a certain item of property by any means necessary—which, I assume, as he undoubtedly did, would include torture and murder. Two days later, he was murdered himself. I have no proof that the two events were connected—he was a man with numerous enemies—but I can hardly be blamed for my suspicion, and my anxiety."

"What was the man's name?" Dupin asked.

"In Paris, he went by the name of Carlo Valdoni. If the police are investigating his death, that is probably the name they have attributed of the victim. His was something of a shadowy presence—he did not go through the formalities normally required of foreign nationals resident in Paris. I cannot be entirely certain, however, that his presence had not been noted by spies of the Sûreté and his real name recorded."

"How did he die?" was Dupin's next question.

"Stabbed with a stiletto, in the style that might be expected of a vendetta killing—but we are talking about a *bravo*, you understand…a man exceedingly skilled with such weaponry himself, and one who had good reason to be wary. An assassin who could kill a man like that, without any apparent struggle, must be reckoned highly skilled in his work."

"Unless he was a friend or relative, who was able to get close to Valdoni without coming under any suspicion of murderous intent," Dupin suggested.

Saint-Germain nodded, although he shared Dupin's ability to make an agreement seem like a flat contradiction. The waiter had reappeared with the bottle of Armagnac, as yet unopened, and three clean glasses. Saint-Germain waited until the bottle had been unsealed and uncorked, and three measures poured out; then he gave the waiter a couple of silver coins and waved away the copper coins offered as change. When the man had gone back inside he said: "The police will undoubtedly jump to the conclusion that it was a vendetta killing; that is why they might not be inclined to invest much time in its investigation. Personally, I have reason to suspect that it was a Neapolitan stiletto rather than a Venetian one."

Dupin nodded in his turn. "What was the item of property that Valdoni was asked to seize from you?" he asked.

"I don't know, exactly—the negotiation with his aspirant client broke down before that item of information was communicated. You'll understand, I think, that the hiring of an assassin can be a delicate business, in diplomatic terms. Once Valdoni discovered that he was unable to accept the commission, he did not want to know any more about it, lest he expose himself to danger—a precaution that seems to have been unavailing—and his sense of honor might have prevented him from telling me the name of his hirer even if he had discovered it. In fact, he told me that he had deliberately refrained from asking, as was his policy. He did, however, tell me that the person who had approached him was a Neapolitan by birth. I presume that he was attempting to emphasize that the threat did not originate Venice—he did not bother to speculate why the person had approached him rather than a fellow countryman, but it might imply that there would have been some hazard in taking the latter course. At any rate, it is a significant detail."

"I assume that you have some other reason for suspecting a Neapolitan connection." The statement was not inflected as if it were a question; Dupin was always confident of his deductions.

"Yes. Again, I have no firm proof, but again, the coincidence of timing is too close to be ignored. The Harmonic Society has lately come into a legacy from a member of Neapolitan origin."

"The Harmonic Society?" This time there was an interrogative inflection. "Not you personally?"

"The terms of the will were quite clear," Saint-Germain said. "All of the movable and immovable property owned by the member in Paris has become the property of the Harmonic Philosophical Society of Paris...but it might be the case that other heirs, to whom immovable properties in Naples and Corsica have reverted, having been subject to some sort of entailment, do not quite understand that I am merely the president of the society…an impression that might have been confirmed by the fact that I had some of the late Monsieur Angelotti's belongings removed from his house in the Faubourg Saint-Denis to my own residence…purely for safe-keeping, you understand…."

I presumed that Dupin did understand, because he did not choose to question the legitimacy of the action in question. Instead, he said: "Tommaso Angelotti? The Marquis de Puységur's friend and one-time collaborator? Surely he died many years ago?"

"I believe that the man I knew as Tommaso Angelotti did work with the Marquis at one time—long before I came to Paris. I hardly knew Puységur, although I'm familiar with his work through his books. I can't really say that I knew Tommaso very well myself, although he made the effort to attend all the important meetings of the society, despite having to be carried everywhere, no longer being able to walk. He *was* very old, and his body was so frail that it's a miracle that he hadn't died long ago, but his mind still seemed sharp. He was our oldest member—although that is not a matter that was publicized, as the Society learned to prize discretion long before I joined its ranks.

"At any rate, I was impressed by Tommaso when I first met him, and was certain that he there was a good deal that I might learn from him. He was the oldest of the handful of the surviving members of the society who had actually met Anton Mesmer and the Comte de Cagliostro—the most prestigious of our founders—and he had been an assiduous enquirer in his day, even though he never wrote a book, and that old rascal Puységur appears to have minimized his contribution to their collaboration in the interests of exaggerating his own. I made an effort to befriend him even before I became President of the Society, as I did with all of the survivors of the Revolutionary Era—by which, of course, I mean the era of Mesmer's great discovery, not the petty political squabble that saw so many good men guillotined by the rabble—and I thought it my duty as President to visit him occasionally following my election."

"Of course you did," said Dupin, a trifle absent-mindedly. "As an assiduous enquirer yourself, especially when matters of inheritance are involved, you would naturally feel obliged to do that. Exactly which item of Signor Angelotti's movable property do you think that the mysterious hirer of thieves and assassins might have been eager to acquire?"

Saint-Germain did not react to the not-so-subtle insult. "I've already told you that I don't know exactly what they're after," he said, taking a considerable gulp of Armagnac. "There are two items that are particularly interesting, however. One is a box with some kind of trick lock, which looks a likely hiding place—and one of the reasons that I've come to you is the hope you might be able to open it without damaging it. I'm still somewhat reluctant to smash it open with an axe or a hammer, although I admit that my patience is wearing thin. The other is a musical instrument that is certainly worth a great deal of money, although I haven't yet been able to obtain an expert evaluation."

"Why would the would-be possessor have waited until now to make the attempt to acquire the item of property, given that it was surely easier to steal it, as it were, at source?" was Dupin's next question, asked in a slightly softer tone.

"Again, I don't know for sure—but I suspect that it wasn't until your punctilious friends at the Palais de Justice notified the heir to his Neapolitan and Corsican properties that anyone in Naples discovered where he had been for the last forty years or so. Carlo Valdoni is by no means the only Italian who is—or was—living in Paris because it was no longer safe for him to live in his homeland, nor the only one who found it convenient to live here under an assumed name."

"Angelotti was a pseudonym?"

"Yes, but neither I nor any other member of the Society knew that until he died, whereupon the reading of his will brought his true identity—or, at least, his real name—to light."

"Why do you make the distinction?" Dupin asked.

"That's the other reason why I need your help. All I know is a name, and there's no one in the Society now who knows any more than I do, all those who might once have been party to his secret having predeceased the unfortunate Tommaso. I have no access to the Sûreté's Archives—but you do."

"And you think that those Archives might contain some relevant information?"

"If any records from the Revolutionary and Imperial eras survive, yes—and I'm sure that they must, given that the Prefecture has always been such an avid hoarder of information. Unlike Carlo, Signor Angelotti was not a *bravo* living beyond the scope of respectable society; the probability is that he completed the necessary formalities, albeit in secret. As a foreign resident of some social standing, and the owner of property abroad, he would have been subject to some kind of monitoring in any case—but I suspect that his relationship with the French authorities might have gone further than that."

Dupin frowned thoughtfully at that, and fell silent. I could not help reacting in his stead.

"You think this Angelotti fellow was a *spy*?" I queried. "You think he was in hiding from his own people because he betrayed them to the French during the Napoleonic Wars—or even before?"

Saint-Germain looked me in the eye and retorted: "I don't know. Nor can I find out, without Dupin's help—and I need to find out, if members of some Neapolitan *camorra* really are after my blood. That's why I'm here."

Dupin remained silent, presumably turning the information he had so far received over and over in his mind, looking at it from every angle, as he was wont to do. He did not toy with his brandy-glass, as I would have done, but he did stare into space, focusing vaguely on the steeple of Saint-Germain des Prés.

I accepted the burden of continuing the interrogation. "Given that you know so little," I said, "and that you probably have enemies as well as friends among the lower orders of Venice and elsewhere, perhaps we ought to consider the possibility that the reason someone wants you dead has nothing to do with the Harmonic Society's recent inheritance. Perhaps, for instance, Mademoiselle Valdemar wants to pay you back for your betrayal?"

Had Saint-Germain not been so desirous of staying on Dupin's good side, for the moment, I think he might have reacted angrily to that. He certainly seemed to be constraining himself as he said: "Doubtless you have heard about Mademoiselle Valdemar's response to the discovery that I helped deceive her from Madame Hanska, to whom she must have poured out her anguish. I can assure you, though, that Jana has no murderous intentions towards me—and that if she had, she certainly would not attempt to hire a Venetian *bravo* to do the job on her behalf. She knows that we are two of a kind, and are inevitably fated to join forces again in the end. As for other enemies—yes, I do have a few, but I can only repeat what I have told you before: I am not nearly as bad a man as Monsieur Dupin suspects me to be, and I do not go through life stirring up murderous resentments wherever I may be. There is, in any case, one more crucial item of evidence that gives me reason to believe that it must be the Angelotti inheritance that has sparked this affair."

"What's that?" Dupin put in, impatiently, evidently annoyed by the fact that Saint-Germain had enough regard for the principles of dramatic suspense to hold back something "crucial" beyond the point at which his narrative seemed to have come to an end.

"Signor Angelotti had a housekeeper named Maddalena—possibly the last survivor of a staff that was once more numerous, although it's equally possible that they've lived *à deux* since his arrival in Paris. For some time, I was convinced that she was a deaf mute; she never said a word when she delivered notes to the Society on his behalf. When I began to call on him at home, however, I discovered that she could hear his instructions—although she never responded to mine—and could also mutter replies, albeit in a seemingly-wordless fashion that was incomprehensible to me. Tommaso explained that, although she was still capable of hearing and speaking—both of which she had once been able to do with perfect fluency—both processes had been gradually distorted over time by some quirk of the nervous system. Although he and she had maintained a near-perfect understanding over the years, she found it direly difficult to make herself comprehensible to others. He seemed genuinely sorrowful about that circumstance, although he always treated the poor woman as a virtual slave rather than a trusted companion.

"At any rate, when I brought a carriage round to Tommaso's house in order to collect some of the possessions left to the Society in his will—which I did very promptly when the terms of the will were communicated to me, for fear that they might not be safe where they were—Maddalena protested very vehemently, and, to begin with, quite incomprehensibly. Much of what she said was mere shrieking, the pitch of her voice shifting in the most remarkable fashion. I tried to calm her with my gaze—which is not without a certain power, and has been known to calm hysterics in the past—but that only seemed to frustrate her. Thinking that it might be better to use my magnetic talents to restore some function to her organs of speech, I set my hand on her brow, and focused my attention carefully.

"It seemed to work—but restoring a measure of her power of speech did not improve her temper in the slightest. She began to address me in what seemed to me to be a curious mixture of blurred French and one of those strange rustic dialects that even civilized Italians have difficulty understanding, which derive from the awkward hybridization of the Latin-descended tongue with some ancient language of a more barbaric slant. I cannot pretend to have absorbed any more than the gist of her tirade, which was still largely inarticulate, but I am perfectly certain that she was trying to prevent my taking the items of property I wanted to remove—particularly the two that I have mentioned.

"When she became convinced of her impotence, she cursed me loudly, roundly and extravagantly...and I do mean that she *cursed* me, rather than merely engaging in colorful blasphemy for its own sake. Were I not an adept, I fear that her curse might even have taken effect—but I am fully in possession of my own magnetic powers, and have no need to be afraid of curses cast by crazy old women."

Dupin scrupulously showed no surprise at what seemed to me to be a remarkable and improbable account of a blatantly immoral series of actions. "What kind of curse?" was my friend's only response.

"She referred, unmistakably, to the evil eye—and I must say that she had the gaze to make such a claim plausible, at least to people of her own sad kind. The words *malocchio* and *jettaura* were both used repeatedly, more than once in association with a third term that I could not grasp at first—I mistook it initially for Grigoryi, which I had just discovered to be Tommaso's real given name, but eventually realized that it must be *egregoroi*—which means…."

"I know what it means," Dupin said, with a frostiness that was more than the mere offence of a man who prided himself on knowing the meanings of a great many esoteric and peculiar terms. I had no idea what the word meant myself, but I had no immediate chance to ask for a clarification.

"Well, there were other words I could recognize too, including *diavolo* and *strix*—and I was almost ready, for a moment, to believe that the old lady *was* a witch, or, at least, that she believed herself to be capable of casting spells. My main concern, however, was to soothe her temper, which I assumed to be based in anxiety. Thinking that she must be afraid of being thrown out of the house where she had lived for half a century, I tried to reassure her that I had no intention of doing so, and that I was quite willing to pay her a wage for continuing in her service as housekeeper, on the society's behalf. Alas, my reassurances only seemed to inflame her ire, and in the end I had to leave—as soon as the carriage was loaded, of course. Perhaps mercifully, she did not attempt to follow me.

"When Carlo came to me, the following day, with the information that someone was willing to pay to recover a certain item of property, I have to admit that my attitude to the old lady became a trifle less sympathetic. I assumed that her newly-loosened tongue must have been given too much exercise. I went back to the house, intending to interrogate her—mainly, of course, to find out what she knew about her master's past. I was too late, alas—the bird had flown. I have no idea where she is now. I'm a fool, I know…I should have interrogated her when I had the chance…."

"You have, of course, considered the possibility that she was the one who tried to hire Valdoni?" Dupin queried.

"How could I overlook something so obvious? It seems unlikely, though. An old serving-woman with communication problems is not the kind of person one would expect to hire a bravo, even if she had the means to pay him—which I doubt, given that I took care to remove all the items of value from the house. I don't doubt that she would do anything possible to recover those items, even though they she has no legal claim to them, but, to be perfectly frank, if she is the one who tried to hire Carlo, then I probably don't have any real reason to be afraid. If, on the other hand, the *camorra* are on my trail…that would be a very different matter. It's difficult to believe that anyone could have reached Paris from Naples in the time between the initial revelation of the terms of the will and my collection of the property, but lawyers can become loose-lipped when they see their paymasters slipping away, and become anxious about the continuity of their income."

Technically, I knew, the terms of Tommaso Angelotti's will should not have been made public until all the heirs had been notified and summoned. Clearly, Saint-Germain's sharp practice was not restricted to his rapid swoop on the property left to the Society of which Angelotti had long been a member—but the property had, after all, been his to claim, at least on behalf of the Society….

"Is it possible," Dupin asked, "that Tommaso, sensing that he had not long to live, had relaxed his customary discretion?"

"Of course," Saint-Germain agreed. "It's even possible—Heaven forbid!—that a member of the Society might be involved. You can doubtless understand why I'm so anxious to clarify the situation."

"Indeed," Dupin affirmed. "Do you know Maddalena's surname?"

"No—only Tommaso's...I mean, *Grigoryi*'s. That was Mazzoli. It means nothing to me." His gaze had sharpened suddenly, as if on the lookout for some hint that the name might mean something to Dupin, but Dupin was too wily to let anything show in his face if it did.

Saint-Germain poured himself a generous measure of Armagnac, and topped up our glasses, although we were some way behind him, having only sipped modestly from the initial ration. The he looked around, scanning the other clients of the *cabaret* and the passers-by in the street, as if searching for a stiletto-wielding assassin. I could not tell whether he was sincerely fearful for his life, or whether he was putting on an act in order to obtain Dupin's help in solving the puzzle.

"Grigoryi's an odd name for an Italian," I observed.

"Less odd in Naples than it would be in Venice," Saint-Germain remarked. "Campania has had a great many over-lords since the colony of Parthenope was founded there by the Greeks, and all of them have left a legacy in terms of surnames and Christian names alike—but it might conceivably be significant that Grigoryi is ultimately derived from *egregoroi*."

That was a chance to ask for enlightenment as to the meaning of the word, but Dupin got in ahead of me. "What letters did the housekeeper bring to the Society on her master's behalf?" he asked.

"Oh, nothing revealing, I fear. When he wanted to attend a meeting, Tommaso would send a note the day before to ask for the necessary assistance. He could still scribble a few lines of script, although he could no longer walk further than a few steps, and his arms would have lacked the strength to propel him far in a wheeled chair even if his fingers had been able to grip the wheel. He required two strong young fellows to carry him from his own armchair to a carriage, and then from the carriage to a chair at the meeting-table—and back again, of course."

"Strong young fellows like the one lurking over there near the church door?" Dupin queried. I followed the direction of his glance, and observed a hulking brute who looked as if he could have carried me, let alone a frail old man, without assistance. For a moment, I thought he might be the murderer commissioned to find and stab Saint-Germain, but then realized that I had the wrong end of the stick, and that I was actually looking at Saint-Germain's bodyguard.

"You can't blame me for not stepping outside without protection," Saint-Germain said, a trifle shamefacedly. There was an ironic note in his voice, however, when he added: "After all, you rarely go abroad without this lusty fellow to defend you in case of need."

In fact, that was not true—Dupin very often went abroad without me, especially in daylight—but I suspected that Saint-Germain was merely attempting to cast aspersions on my worth as a defender. The aspersions in question were not entirely unjustified—but I took what comfort I could from the supposition that Saint-Germain probably did not know that Dupin was a good deal stronger and more physically able than his relatively slender frame implied, more competent to serve as my bodyguard than I was to serve as his.

"Within his home, though," Dupin said, "Signor Angelotti had no one left to help him than this Maddalena?"

"I doubt that he traveled far, given that he seemed to be reduced to living in a single room," Saint-Germain said, "and although the faithful Maddalena was probably no more than a decade younger than he was, she came from sturdy peasant stock. Her muscles did not seem to me to have weakened with age, however addled her faculties might have been."

"I shall need to see that room," Dupin said, decisively, "as well as the items that you removed from it...on the Society's behalf. We shall start with the latter, I think...without delay."

As soon as he had spoken, Dupin drained his glass. Mine still had a generous measure in it—the measure that Saint-

Germain had poured while topping up his own glass—and so did the Mesmerist's. Neither of us made any immediate attempt to empty the glasses.

"That's not…," Saint-Germain began, presumably intending to say that he wanted Dupin to go to the Prefecture first, to obtain whatever information was available there—but he thought better of it, obviously realizing that, since he had asked for help, he was not in a position to dictate the manner in which it was offered. He stopped, and nodded his head meekly. Then he picked up his glass, and began taking rapid sips, intent on downing the liquid rapidly, if not in an uncouth fashion.

I copied him. The bottle was still half full, but Saint-Germain simply grabbed it and signaled to his bodyguard, to whom he handed it. "We'll take a fiacre," he said to Dupin, "even though it's not far. Time is of the essence."

As if on cue, a wandering violinist playing to the customers in a restaurant on the far side of the street ran his fingers down the neck of his instrument to contrive what I now knew to be a *glissando*. It was as if he, or Fate, were informing us that we had just taken a step into the unknown, where time and being might become unhinged.

At the time, that did not seem to me to be an uninviting prospect; an adventure, I thought, would provide a useful distraction from the oppressions of late August—and for once, I would not have to dig into my own pocket to pay the fare that would ferry us to the shore of mystery.

CHAPTER THREE
THE BOX AND THE CELLO

The fiacre did not, in fact, have far to go; had Dupin and I been on our own, we would certainly have walked, and I suspect that the fake Comte might well have done likewise, but now that we had formed a company of sorts, our reluctant client seemed to feel there were certain ceremonies best observed. It was, however, Saint-Germain's bodyguard—whom he had introduced to us as Donatien—who paid off the coachman while the master of the house rang the doorbell. That too struck me as slightly odd, but we were in the ancient heart of the Faubourg after which the charlatan had named himself, where aristocratic practises were strictly observed, especially by those who were only aping aristocracy. True Comtes did not open their own front doors; they had staff to do that for them.

In truth, the Comte's town house was not very grand, especially compared to its imposing neighbors, but it had a coaching entrance, a courtyard and stables, and three stories above ground as well as a cellar below. I was not in a position to count his valets, grooms and housemaids, let alone his kitchen staff, but I was impressed by his English butler, whose presence and attitude signified that the charlatan was up to date with the Faubourg's very latest fashions. The butler's name was Whalen, and his deferential manner was impeccable, but he did give the impression that if any common-or-garden gang of thieves or murderers had the temerity to break into the house that constituted his petty empire, they would meet a stern and educated defense.

Saint-Germain did not stand on ceremony; the butler showed us into a reception-room, as convention demanded, but we hardly lingered there for thirty seconds before the Comte was leading us upstairs himself, to inspect the loot that he had already plundered from the legacy confided to the Harmonic Philosophical Society of Paris by its oldest member.

The objects in question had presumably been transported directly from the carriage that had brought them here to an unused guest-room, where they had been laid down ready for closer examination and sorting—a process that had begun, but was by no means concluded, to judge by the disorder in which the objects remained.

There was a secretaire with a roll-top lid, whose drawers and pigeon-holes had obviously been searched—including the standard drawer with the "secret" lock, whose trick had long since become common knowledge. There was also a pair of fine Louis Quinze dining-chairs, a polished wooden table devoid of drawers or secrets bearing a porcelain flower-vase and a few other knick-knacks, a pendulum clock of the kind called a "grandfather clock" in England, a quilted armchair, and a number of paintings, stacked in series, with their backs facing the room. All these objects were pushed back against the wall or the bed-alcove as if by way of dismissal, leaving the center of the carpet free for two items that had obviously come to monopolize the attentions of the searcher.

The larger of the two was a musical instrument case, whose lid had been thrown back to expose the instrument within, which was a large violoncello—a "bass cello", if my rather precarious mastery of orchestral nomenclature could be trusted. It looked to me like an old and very fine instrument; there was a bow neatly attached by a pair of grips to the inside of the lid, and a block of rosin in a compartment designed to contain it. The inner surface of the lid was also fitted with a series of pockets, into which musical scores might be tucked, but the pockets were empty.

The smaller of the two objects that had retained their new owner's attention, perhaps more than the other, was an ornately-carved wooden box with a rounded lid. It was too big to be a jewel-box and too small to be a trunk, although it had something of the air of both. Remarkably, it had no keyhole, and it was very difficult to see whether the lid was fitted to the body of the box, the revealing crack and the hinges being entirely masked by neatly-carved fern-like leaves and little flowers of indeterminate species. Indeed, the crack might not have been visible at all to the casual gaze had an attempt not been made to prise the lid open with the blade of a dagger, whose tip had broken off within the slender gap thus opened up. Saint-Germain had told us that he was reluctant to smash the box open with a hammer or an axe, but his patience had obviously buckled under the strain even before he decided to swallow his pride and approach Dupin, and he might not have been far removed from such a drastic step.

"There must be some kind of hidden catch, or a combination of pressure-points," the false Comte said to Dupin, "but I'm damned if I can find it. If you can open the box, we might find something inside that will tell us what this is all about."

Dupin knelt down to inspect the box more closely, considering it from several different angles, but did not seem to be in any particular hurry to solve the puzzle. He did pick the box up, however, and move it from side to side. A muffled sound came from within, like that of a soft but solid object shifting, but I could not tell from the sound alone what shape the object might be.

After twenty seconds or so of dutiful peering and shaking, Dupin set the box down again, and moved on to inspect the cello and its bulky case with similarly minute care.

"Did Signor Angelotti—I mean Signor Mazzoli—play this instrument?" he asked.

"Once upon a time, I dare say," Saint-Germaine replied, "but it must have been a very long time ago—his hands were so stricken with arthritis that he could barely grip a cup or a pen without using both of them. Even if he were able to wield the bow, he surely could not have picked out notes on the strings. I doubt that he would have been able to do that for at least thirty years—perhaps since the beginning of the century. The instrument must have been of considerable sentimental value, though, else he'd have sold it. It *is* worth a good deal of money, is it not?"

"Probably," Dupin said. "I'm no judge of prices. You'll have to consult a dealer if you want an estimate of its worth in commercial terms—but I can speak for the quality of the workmanship, which is excellent. Have you attempted to play it?"

"Me? No. I was taught to play the piano in my youth, and showed a certain dexterity, but my vocation was magical—or at least Mesmeric—rather than musical. Do you play?"

"I had lessons once," Dupin said, vaguely. "On the violin rather than the cello—but the principle is the same."

"Would you like to try it out?" the Mesmerist asked, a trifle sarcastically.

"No," said Dupin. "Is there anyone in the Society who has the skill?" I assumed that he was wondering whether there was anyone among the members of the Harmonic Society—other than Saint-Germain, of course—who might be willing to steal from the association in order to acquire personal possession of such a precious object.

"We *are* a Harmonic Society," Saint-Germain replied, retaining a mocking irony in his voice, "but I fear that we're more concerned with the music of the spheres and the harmonies of souls than symphonies and chamber music. I doubt that you'd be able to assemble an effective string quartet from the membership, let alone a functional orchestra, although there are numerous music-lovers among us who delight in hosting recitals."

"You mentioned before that Grigoryi Mazzoli knew Cagliostro," Dupin said, out of the blue. "Do you have any reason to suspect a connection between Cagliostro and the cello?"

"No, do you?" Saint-Germain was quick to counter—but then, I suspect, remembered that, in his imposture as the Comte de Saint-Germain, he was supposed to have been acquainted with Cagliostro himself. Swiftly, he went on: "If only my old friend and protégé were still here…but France has ever been unkind to the greater number of its Italian refugees. Anyway, you're the man who possesses the only copy of *Les Harmonies de l'enfer* known to exist in Paris, which must be one of the copies Cagliostro had printed and bound, so you're as capable as I am of guessing whether the instrument has more harmonic significance than any other of its sort. Do you know something about Tommaso Angelotti's work with Puységur that makes you suspect that he was interested in musical magic?"

"He was an assiduous member of your Society," Dupin reminded him, mildly. "You even claim to have befriended him. If he had some such interest, surely you'd be aware of it? Or perhaps not. If he did have any secrets of that sort, is there anyone apart from you to whom he might have confided them?"

Saint-Germain bit his lip, perhaps regretting the fact that he had not contrived to get to know Tommaso Angelotti a little better, or perhaps experiencing chagrin at the thought that the old man had kept secrets from him without his even having realized that there were secrets to be kept. "Perhaps…." he answered, vaguely.

I expected Dupin to seize upon the obvious evasion, but he did not. "Giuseppe Balsamo, alias the Comte de Cagliostro, died in 1795," he murmured, pensively. "If Angelotti knew him, it must have been in Italy, before Balsamo came to Paris. Do you know when Angelotti joined your Society, exactly?"

"Not until 1817," Saint-Germain replied, "although he had come to Paris some years before that, if I'm taking the right inference from remarks he made in my presence."

"And how old was he when he died?"

"Ninety-four—the will revealed that he was born in 1752. That makes Cagliostro ten years his senior, I believe…but even if they were only acquainted in Italy, as relatively young men, before either of them settled in Paris, the Prefecture will surely have a record of any connection that existed between them, given the close watch that Louis XVI's spies kept on Cagliostro."

"Perhaps they have," Dupin mused. Then he began to move around the room, inspecting the odd items of furniture, opening the case of the clock, tilting back the paintings one by one to inspect their faces, and finally riffling through the papers exposed in the open drawers of the secretaire. He paused for some time over the various papers that Saint-Germain had removed from the drawers, paying particular attention to a number of musical scores, all of which were printed and of seemingly recent origin—too recent, I judged, for Mazzoli's arthritic fingers ever to have played any of them, on any instrument whatsoever.

I presumed that it was the seeming incongruity of the scores that had attracted Dupin's attention, and was pleased to notice, on edging closer and looking over his shoulder, that they included at least one *nocturne* by Chopin and another by the English composer John Field. Perhaps, I thought, they would remind Dupin of his vague promise to take a little more notice of such things.

When Dupin eventually turned back to Saint-Germain, it was to ask: "Where's the piano? Was it too large, or not sufficiently valuable, to be worth transporting?"

"There was no piano in Tommaso's house," Saint-Germain reported. "Not in the room where he lived, nor in any other. I would have noticed—as I said, I can play a piano. I have one of my own, if you'd like I look at it—but I presume you're asking because some of that sheet music is for sonatas that require a piano as well as a cello, and other pieces are for the piano alone."

"Indeed," Dupin admitted.

"As he couldn't play the cello any longer, the music was presumably of purely theoretical interest to him—it might as well have been scored for an entire orchestra. Anyway, I've looked through all of the papers in the desk, and there's nothing of any use. What about the box? Have you ever seen one like it?"

"No," Dupin confessed. "Given time, I might well be able

to locate the hidden catch—but I rather doubt that what your friend Valdoni was hired to steal is in there."

"Why do you say that?"

"Because Signor Angelotti—Mazzoli—had arthritic fingers. If there had ever been anything in the box to which he needed ready access, he would surely have removed it while he was still capable of gaining access to it. Whatever he left in there, he was either prepared to forsake, or prepared to entrust to the stronger and nimbler fingers of his faithful Maddalena. Maddalena appears to have been taken completely by surprise by your sudden visit, and to have become angry in consequence, but if whatever is in the box had been of crucial importance, and she had access to it, she would probably have been able to find an opportunity to remove it while you were searching the house—whatever is in the box is small enough to slip into a pocket or secrete elsewhere. That inclines me to suspect that the cello is the more crucial object, and the more likely target of the intended theft."

"That's plausible," Saint-Germain conceded. "On the other hand, Monsieur Dupin, I suspect that you're itching to know what's in the box as much as I am, simply because it's so ingeniously sealed—so there's no point in trying to deflect my attention away from it."

Dupin shrugged his shoulders, as if to say that Saint-Germain was welcome to his futile suspicions. He did bend down to pick the box up again, however, and shake it gently for a second time, placing his ear closer to the side in order to measure the timbre of the muted rattle within.

"Hmm!" he said, finally—and put the box down again.

"What do you mean, *hmm!*" said Saint-Germain, exasperatedly. "If you think you know what it is, tell me."

"I'm a logician, not a conjuror," Dupin retorted. "Given time to experiment and think, I could probably discover the catch, but if this matter is urgent—and I'm beginning to believe your assurance that it is—there are other things that we ought do first. I shall visit the Prefecture first thing in the morning, but if I'm to be properly forearmed, I need to see Angelotti's house first. Shall we use your carriage, or would you rather send someone for a fiacre?"

"It will be quicker to fetch a fiacre, since we're in a hurry," Saint-Germain said—and went to give the order.

I moved rapidly to Dupin's side. "Do you know what's in the box?" I asked him, in a whisper.

"I could make a guess, based on its apparent weight, texture and dimensions," Dupin admitted, "but it would only be a guess—the solution to the mystery cannot be deemed solved until the lid is actually opened. I can also make an educated guess, alas, as to why Grigoryi Mazzoli's Neapolitan heir might be so anxious to get his hands on his personal property, if that really is what is happening here. As the housekeeper has already informed Saint-Germain, indirectly, this matter has something to do with witchcraft and *egregoroi*. We need to find out why Mazzoli fled Naples, and why he joined the Harmonic Society. Puységur obviously could not help him to achieve his goal, nor Saint-Germain…perhaps no one could…but he does not seem to have given up on his hopes entirely, and someone evidently has the intention of taking over where he left off."

"Do you believe that Saint-Germain really restored Maddalena's power of speech?" I asked. "Surely that's just bluster, like his nonsense about having tutored Cagliostro in the idle of the last century?"

"He might be a charlatan, but he is a capable Mesmerist," Dupin replied. "Even Puységur had some success in that regard, though never as much as he claimed—and you've seen for yourself what skilled practitioners like Monsieur Dupotet and Mademoiselle Valdemar are able to do. Perhaps Saint-Germain only helped the old woman to overcome some kind of psychological block…but even if his gesture was purely symbolic, it could well have been very effective. If she really is his enemy, though, or his enemy's instrument, increasing her capacity for action might not have been a wise move."

"You mean that the curse she tried to put on him might yet

take effect?"

"If she really did try to curse him—but what he told us leaves open the slight possibility that she was actually trying to warn him, and that any curse that might afflict him might come from another direction entirely."

"From the object in the box, perhaps?" I guessed.

"Perhaps," he admitted, grudgingly.

"But you do think Saint-Germain is in danger?" I queried.

"Probably—perhaps deadly danger, in spite of his Mesmeric abilities and his army of would-be protectors. Signor Mazzoli's life was presumably in danger throughout his long life, given the extent of his discretion—and we might be in danger of harm ourselves if we ask too many questions, let alone obtain the right answers."

I was slightly taken aback by that, but the question I put in response was rhetorical. "But we're going to ask the questions anyway, aren't we?"

That won a rare smile from my friend. "We certainly are," he said. "And I thank you for the unhesitating *we*."

Saint-Germain came back in then. "The cab will be at the door in a matter of minutes," he said. "If you're really determined not to make an attempt on the box tonight, we might as well go down to meet it."

"If you'd allow me to take the box away," Dupin suggested, "I could work on it at my leisure at home, once I've cast an eye over Signor Angelotti's place of residence."

The false Comte laughed. "You can't expect that of me, Monsieur Dupin," he said. "If you can open it in my presence, all well and good—I'll be duly grateful to you—but if you think I'm going to hand it over...I can play the trial and error game myself, and if I get bored, I still have other daggers, not to mention a hatchet and a sledgehammer. This is *my* mystery, remember—not yours."

"It's *ours* now," said Dupin, mildly, as he left the room and went to the stair-head. "A mystery shared is a mystery divided, and having brought this one to my attention, you had best work with me, for you certainly do not want to be in awkward competition with the man most likely to reach a profitable solution."

"If I did not need you to ask questions at the Prefecture on my behalf…." Saint-Germain began, resentfully.

"But you do," Dupin told him, firmly. "And I suspect that, in the end, you will be grateful that you swallowed your pride and sought me out."

I trusted my friend's suspicion, of course—but Saint-Germain seemed to be in two minds about it.

CHAPTER FOUR
TOMMASO ANGELOTTI'S PARIS HOME

The house at whose door the fiacre pulled up was a small one, by Parisian standards. It had no courtyard or stable, and no concierge's lodge. It had only two stories; it had obviously been designed to accommodate the family of an *ouvrier* devoid of servants. Saint-Germain had a bunch of keys that gave us admittance to the house. I noticed that the main door had no less than three locks—which was by no means typical of *ouvriers'* cottages, even in crime-ridden Paris.

Saint-Germain gave the coachman a coin and told him to wait—an instruction that did not seem to displease the fellow at all, for he had already wrapped himself up in his overcoat and scarf—the night was perfectly clear and the temperature had fallen quite steeply once darkness had fallen. He did not stretch himself out on his bench immediately, though; before going to sleep he had to see to his horse. He pulled a bucket out from beneath his seat and set off to fill it at the tap at the end of the street.

Saint-Germain was careful; he sent Donatien into the house first, with instructions to check every room and make sure that no one was inside. That did not take long, and once the place had been guaranteed safe Saint-Germain instructed his man to remain on the doorstep, standing guard.

Apart from the tiny kitchen, there was only one large room on the ground floor, which was obviously the one in which the house's principal resident had spent his time once his mobility was restricted. There was a long, comfortably-upholstered settee as well as a rickety four-poster bed, a wardrobe, a book-case, a sideboard, a commode—in the English rather than the French sense of the term—and a wash-basin. The papered walls seemed a trifle bleak without the paintings that had hung there—the patches from which they had been withdrawn were clearly visible, testifying to the extent to which the rest of the paper had been darkened by the smoke of cheap candles and lamps burning poor-quality oil. The carpet was even filthier. Tommaso Angelotti had certainly not lived in luxury, but had not been tempted by that circumstance to sell the expensive cello he could no longer play.

It was obvious that Saint-Germain had left little of value behind when he had swooped like a hawk to perform an initial clearance "on the Society's behalf." Even so, Dupin began to move around the room very carefully, inspecting everything. As might be expected, he paid particular attention to the books in the cabinet.

"Did you take anything from here for your own library?" he asked Saint-Germain.

"No," the mesmerist replied. "Everything I took was still in the room where you inspected it; the books on those shelves are old, but not particularly valuable. I don't read Italian fluently, but I can decipher titles—and the majority are, in any case, in French. Considering that he was a one-time acquaintance of Cagliostro and long-term member of the Harmonic Society, his tastes in reading seem to have been distinctly prosaic."

"Not a single title by Puységur," Dupin observed, as if in agreement—and passed on to the sideboard. He was in no hurry, although the hour was now very late indeed, and I felt rather drowsy.

"This is futile," Saint-Germain put in, when he could bear the tension no longer. "Maddalena's reaction made it quite obvious that whatever she was trying to protect was among the items I took away—if not the box with the trick lock, then the cello."

"I'd be more convinced of that had you actually understood what she was saying," Dupin told him, as he sorted through the clothes in the wardrobe. Finally, though, he seemed satisfied, and declared that it was time to look upstairs.

There were three rooms upstairs, but two of them were very small, and almost bare. The room in which Maddalena had presumably slept, however, was very different—just as cluttered, in fact, as the room downstairs must have been before Saint-Germain had mounted his raid.

"I'm not at all sure," Saint-Germain said, uneasily, "that anything here would be counted as part of Mazzoli's bequest. The servant's personal possessions are, presumably, her own."

"That's very scrupulous of you," Dupin said, "But I don't intend to take anything away. If she comes back, she'll find everything here as she left it—assuming that you observed the same principle when you searched it yourself."

"I did," Saint-Germain said. "She doesn't seem to have taken much with her, does she?"

"Not from here," Dupin said, with typical scrupulousness.

"You think she took something from one of the other rooms?"

"Perhaps. Her decision presumably depended on whether she went of her own free will, and how much of a hurry she was in. There are, however, far too many things conspicuous by their absence for her to have taken them all, or even a substantial fraction."

"A piano, for instance?"

"Not necessarily, but possibly. I was thinking of books and, more importantly, papers. I fear that Signor Mazzoli might have thought twice about the terms of his legacy after making his will—unfortunately for you, in more ways than one. The very heart of that legacy seems to be missing. Either he decided to entrust it to someone else, or he destroyed it."

"No," said Saint-Germain, flatly. "He wouldn't have destroyed it—he wasn't that kind of man. Indeed, I find it hard to believe that he would have let anything truly precious out of his immediate custody, even after he lost the ability to handle it. Whatever the heir to the entailed property might want from Tommaso's Paris effects, I believe that it was here, in this house—and is now in mine. There is no other possible reason why Carlo Valdoni would have been asked to force me to give it up."

"That judgment assumes that whoever attempted to hire Valdoni knew where the item in question was. They might have simply jumped to the conclusion that, since it was not here when they came in search of it, you must have removed it. If someone else has it, then you might not be the only person in danger, and it would be as well if we could identify the person in question before anyone else does. If there is such an individual, he or she might not know what it is that has been given to them, or how dangerous it might be to have it."

I assumed that Dupin was probably exercising his pedantic obsession. Saint-Germain seemed to think so too, but he condescended to speculate. "I believe that Tommaso was in communication with the Baron Du Potet," he said, reluctantly.

"Dupotet?" I queried, rendering the name in the less pretentious fashion that Dupin invariably employed. "I didn't know that he was a member of the Harmonic Society."

"As the membership list is supposed to be secret," Saint-Germain countered, "I would be disappointed if you did."

Dupin seemed less surprised than disappointed. "I can understand why Angelotti might have preferred the collaboration of a Baron rather than a mere Comte," he observed, "although the Baron's musical interests were probably more crucial than his dubious title. If Angelotti—Mazzoli, that is—gave his books and papers to Dupotet, in order to cement some sort of collaboration...."

"Perhaps he did," Saint-Germain snapped. I could see that he was annoyed by the possibility, presumably because he had had no inkling of it, although he must have been cultivating Dupotet as assiduously as he had cultivated Angelotti, in order to recruit him as a member of the Society and thus put a claim on his presently-unparalleled prestige as a Mesmerist. "But one thing of which I'm certain is that Dupotet didn't try to hire Carlo, or kill him. That was a Neapolitan. If it wasn't Maddalena...."

Dupin cut him off. "Yes, of course," he said, "we must find Maddalena, urgently—and if we find her, we must also persuade her to tell us what she knows, if she is still able to do so. In the meantime, I must discover whatever I can in the Prefecture's Archives. That will not be easy, by any means, but I know a man who can help me—fortunately, the Prefecture is as careful to conserve its clerks as it is to conserve its documents."

"Help *us*, you mean," said Saint-Germain. "I'm coming with you."

"Help me to help you," Dupin corrected him. "And I'm afraid that your accompanying me is out of the question. There are matters of delicate diplomacy and confidentiality at issue here. That I have access to the Archives is a rare privilege; it is not one that can be extended, even to my friend, let alone to the president of a politically dubious organization. You may be sure, however, that I will tell you everything that I am permitted to reveal, once I have learned it myself—just as you will undoubtedly communicate to me anything that you discover while I am otherwise occupied."

Saint-Germain did not bother to dispute that his was a politically dubious organization. It had deliberately made itself so in the long-gone days when Napoleon had not yet become emperor, by cultivating a culture of esotericism and secrecy. Its members then had been mostly aristocrats and scholars, who had every reason to be afraid of the Terror, but who had also had reason to fear the scorn of an Academic establishment that had turned against animal magnetism in no uncertain terms—and the Society had not forsaken that esotericism when the political and intellectual climate had changed, thus condemning itself to perpetual suspicion and surveillance, under the Restoration as under the Empire, and under Louis-Philippe as under Charles X.

Nor did Saint-Germain bother to voice any doubt he had that Dupin would tell him everything that it was permissible for him to tell—although he obviously suspected that what Dupin and his friends at the Prefecture might consider "permissible" would fall far short of what he would dearly like to know. He had known what a diabolical kind of bargain he was making when he had first accosted us at the *cabaret*.

What Saint-Germain actually said, to express his barely-concealed resentment, was: "And what am I supposed to do while you root around in the Prefecture's vaults for the information that might save my life?"

"You could work on the problem of the box," Dupin suggested, with a hint of irony. "You'd probably be better employed, though, once the morning is sufficiently well-advanced, in visiting the Baron Du Potet and enquiring after any books and papers that Tommaso Angelotti might have entrusted to him—especially musical scores. If you can persuade Du Potet to hand them over, so much the better, but at the very least, you need to find out everything he knows about the goals of your mutual friend's research, and any plans they might have made to carry that research forward. My friend will be happy to keep you company—perhaps, when you've finished with the Baron, you could give him a tour of the Society's premises, and introduce him to those of its secrets you're permitted to reveal."

CHAPTER FIVE
KEEPING SAINT-GERMAIN COMPANY

When we left the house in the Faubourg Saint-Denis, dawn was already beginning to tint the eastern sky. I was surprised to see it, because the hours of darkness seemed to have flown by. The temperature was as low as it was going to get, but it still seemed uncomfortably warm to me. There did not seem to be a breath of wind to relieve the dull pressure of the atmosphere, and the mere anticipation of yet another hot day made my head ache slightly.

Saint-Germain's bodyguard had become drowsy while standing guard at the front door, but he roused himself the moment we opened the door. The fiacre's coachman was fast asleep on his bench, swathed in his cloak and scarf—although I could not understand the necessity—and had to be prodded awake.

While Saint-Germain was waking the coachman, Dupin set off walking southwards. I was momentarily in a quandary as to whether to follow him or not, but when I took a step forward he signaled for me to remain with Saint-Germain. The latter called out to tell him that it would be safer to stay with us while the cab took him to the Île de la Cité, but Dupin merely waved a hasty refusal and plunged ahead on foot, almost at a trot. In the meantime, Saint-Germain ordered the coachman to take him back home, where he presumably intended to eat breakfast before setting off to see Dupotet.

"No one, as yet, has put a price on his head," Saint-Germain muttered, as he watched Dupin draw away. "I suppose he thinks he'll be safer if he's not in my company."

"Had that been his reason for going southwards on foot," I said, "he would have taken me with him."

Saint-Germain looked me up and down in a fashion that was less than complimentary. "I suppose he would," he admitted. "He seems to value your acquaintance, although I have no idea why."

"There's no need to be insulting," I told him. "If you don't want my company, I'll be glad to walk myself—there's no price on my head either."

"I'm sorry," he said, pushing me up into the fiacre. "I dare say that you'll be useful somehow—and Dupin obviously wanted you to stay with me. Since I've asked for his help, I suppose I ought to do as he says...in the matter of investigating the possibility that Tommaso handed on his work to the Baron Du Potet, that is."

"Is he the only possible recipient?" I asked, as I settled myself as comfortably as possible against the meager cushions in the back of the fiacre, taking the seat opposite Saint-Germain while Donatien sat down beside his master.

"Yes, alas. It pains me to admit it, but it's not completely impossible that my acquaintance with Tommaso didn't serve to give him the utmost confidence in my talents as a Mesmerist... although I'm very confident that there are very few members of the Society whose talents can match mine, let alone exceed them."

"But Dupotet is one? I must admit that on the one occasion when I saw him at work, he didn't have any conspicuous success."

"I remember. You went to see him at the Saltpêtrière when Collyer was intercepted by Jana Valdemar—but that was hardly a fair test of his capacity. I will admit that he is flawed, particularly in terms of his social ambition, which seems of late to have become overweening, but he is capable of remarkable feats of magnetism. Tommaso would have recognized that. I must admit, though, that he's not the kind of man I would have chosen as a collaborator. Too self-involved, and too self-important."

"You'll forgive me, I hope, if say that you put me in mind of a pot complaining of the blackness of a kettle."

"Will I? I suppose so. From where you sit, the Baron and I must look like cats of a very similar stripe, and I suppose that I've been enthusiastic to claim him as a collaborator of sorts in the work of the Society...but I've been forced to exercise a great deal of persuasive flattery in achieving that end. There's a sense in which it's easier to dupe a man like Du Potet than to win his honest co-operation. Dupin was hopelessly optimistic to think that he might help with the *lampion* trick he played on Jana, although Chapelain might conceivably have done so. It was always much more my sort of exploit than theirs—I did him a favor by standing in, and paid the cost in term's of Jana's affection and esteem. He really ought to be more grateful—and he hasn't said a word of thanks for the copy of *The Mad Trist* I found for him. Did he tell you what he thought of it?"

"He never read it," I said, perhaps a little too casually. "He gave it to Stephen Coningsby."

"He did *what*?" Saint-Germain seemed genuinely astonished, and quite appalled.

I tried hard to read the expression on his face, but the dawn had not yet produced daylight enough for me to see it very clearly. I could not tell whether he was simply amazed that a book collector like Dupin should part with a rare item so casually, or whether he was disappointed that the curse he had hoped to inflict on the book's ultimate recipient was no longer hanging over Dupin's head...or whether, perhaps he had taken the inference that Dupin must have believed that the book really was cursed, and had therefore hastened to get rid of it—which would, in truth, have been a truly astonishing revelation.

"I read it," I said, mildly. "An interesting text in its way— but not quite Dupin's cup of tea. He reads so omnivorously that he's tolerably familiar with the modern novel, but his primary interest as a collector is in works of esoteric philosophy...as yours is, and presumably Du Potet's too."

Saint-Germain apparently needed time to think about that—which was perhaps as well, as the fiacre was becoming caught up in the heavy traffic in the vicinity of Les Halles, where the markets were still in the process of receiving and laying out their produce. Because it was August, there were more carts than usual, and they were far more copiously loaded. It was almost impossible for carriages to move about in central Paris at certain hours even in the winter, but August was the worst month of all. It was difficult to see what could be done about that without tearing large sections of the city down and running a series of radial boulevards from the outskirts to the core—something that I thought unlikely to happen in my lifetime.

Saint-Germain thumped on the vehicle's front partition and shouted a catalogue of complaints at the coachman, the gist of which was that any fiacre-driver worth his salt ought to know how to avoid traffic jams, or at least to be able to thread his way through them.

The coachman offered an inarticulate apology. My sympathies were with him; I had enough experience of driving in Paris to know how inextricable the traffic became one entanglement set in. The traders in the market, avid to make the most of the temporary abundance of stock, believed that they had a moral entitlement to every inch of display-space they could find and claim—and in the heat of competitions with their rivals, they seemed blissfully unaware of the paradoxical aspect of their intrusion into the roadway, which made it exceedingly difficult for their customers to reach them.

"What does *egregoroi* mean?" I asked Saint-Germain, in order start the conversation going again. "I know that *jettatura* and *malocchio* both refer to the curse of the evil eye, with which you thought Maddalena was attempting to afflict you, and I know that *diavolo* means the Devil and *strix* means witch—but I've heard the word *egregoroi* before."

"It's Greek in origin," Saint-Germain informed me, evidently glad to show off his superiority in matters of abstruse occult lore. "As a plural, it crops up in the *Septuagint*, in a particularly gnomic passage of *Lamentations*, and also in Greek versions of the *Apocrypha*, where it seems to refer to the parents of the equally mysterious *nephilim*. Scholars of your language usually translate it as *watcher*, but the same scholars tend to translate *nephilim* as *giants*, which is absurd. At any rate, the reference remains stubbornly unclear, although that's probably where Dupin has run across it.

"In more recent occult writings, in which it's usually singular and Frenchified as *egregore*, the term has acquired a more specific meaning...or to be strictly accurate, two overlapping meanings. The one more closely associated with the notion of the evil eye refers to the supposed power possessed by certain individuals to establish a kind of psychic link with others, by means of which vital energy can be stolen: a form of energetic predation or parasitism—or, if you prefer, psychic vampirism.

"Some modern scholars believe that's how the power of the evil eye actually works: that the person gifted with the magical power of sight weakens and destroys his or her victim by siphoning off vital energy. You'll be glad to know, however, that Maddalena's attempt to curse me seems to have misfired; I feel quite undiminished. I am, as I mentioned, adept enough in magnetism to be more than a match for any Campanian hedge-witch...."

"No doubt," I said. "And the other meaning?"

"Modern occult scholars also use the term to refer to a new entity resulting from a psychic linkage between two or more minds, contending that the entity in question becomes separate from its units—a whole not only greater than its parts but independent of them, capable of growing stronger, perhaps to the point that the individuals incorporated with it become mere puppets, or individual cells within an organism. That sort of egregore is said to be capable of *possessing* its victims, like a demon, moving the focus of its attention from one to another at will, while managing transfers of energy between them.

Although its principal quotidian effect is to drain its hosts—that kind of independent egregore apparently requires a lot of psychic energy for its own maintenance—it can employ particular magical means, on occasion, to extend its scope considerably."

"Musical magic?" I queried.

"Quite possibly. That kind of entity is still a kind of vampire, I suppose, but one that's disembodied, or in possession of multiple bodies."

"So, if Maddalena linked the term with the evil eye, what do you suppose she was trying to do to you?"

"I'm not sure. My initial assumption was that she was claiming to be an egregore, although she might have been threatening to deliver me into the power of one…but the latter seems unlikely. Given the multiple meanings that can be attached to the term, it's difficult to know exactly what she meant—although it does imply that she has some esoteric knowledge of magic, given that *egregoroi* is a word with which even educated men like you are unfamiliar." Saint-Germain seemed genuinely uncertain, as if he had not given the question any particular attention until I raised it explicitly.

"Is it possible," I asked, following up on a suggestion that Dupin had made, "that she wasn't trying to curse you at all, but merely trying to warn you about a curse associated with the cello…or the mysterious object in the box?"

He looked me in the eyes, as if probing with his Mesmeric gaze, but it was too gloomy for his stare to be effective, even in a purely psychological sense. "I don't think so," he said. "She was so *angry*. I believe that she really was trying to put a curse me…but I think she was also frightened…and it's possible, I suppose, that my own anxieties caused me to misinterpret the situation…. I wish I knew what was in that box! Dupin's deliberately tormenting me, you know, by refusing to try to open it."

"I doubt that," I said, not entirely honestly, "but the fact that there's something hidden from us shouldn't deflect our attention from the object that isn't. Whatever is in the box, we need to know where the cello fits in."

"I dare say that we do." he countered, warily. "It pains me to admit it, but I'm at a disadvantage there, not merely with respect to Dupin but perhaps to you too, if you've read *Les Harmonies de l'enfer*, or even heard a second-hand account of its contents from Dupin. You might well know more about the supposed scope and methods of musical magic than I do."

In fact, I had never read the book in question, and Dupin had always been vague in referring to its contents—but I was reluctant to admit that to Saint-Germain. "I'm not sure that Dupin would approve of my discussing his secrets with you," I said, painfully aware of the lameness of the excuse.

Saint-Germain pulled a face, expressive of disgust—the sun was up now, and I had no difficulty in reading the expression. "Secrets!" he said. "Everyone is obsessed with secrecy—but that didn't prevent Cagliostro from having the manuscript printed. Keep it to yourself, then, if you feel you must. There's probably nothing new you can tell me, anyway. Do you suppose that the pseudonymous Abbé Apollonius was the only crazed neo-Pythagorean mystic who developed ideas in that direction? There were probably half a dozen in Averoigne alone—and he doubtless communicated with others as mad as he was, even if he never gave them his manuscript to read. I may not know the details, but I probably know the broad outlines as well as you do."

"Probably," I conceded. I was simply being honest, but he seemed to take the interjection as a challenge.

"Music and mathematics, in mystical combination, are the ordering forces of the world," he said, bitterly, "their laws being responsible for keeping the dream-dimensions, especially the nightmarish ones, from confusion with the supposedly-solid universe of perception. In that capacity, their harmonies oppose and frustrate the dire work of the Crawling Chaos that threatens to dissolve the entire universe…and also keep at bay the predatory entities that Dupin called the Dwellers of the Thresholds when he convinced poor Jana that the evil eye was well and truly upon her. *That*'s where the music is supposed to fit in, isn't it?—as the best instrument for sealing, or breaking down, the boundaries...except that you might not be well-advised to assume that it has charms to soothe the savage breast of anything that slips through a breach that leads to a nightmare dimension...."

It was difficult to know how seriously he intended the final remarks—but that was not the problem that preoccupied me, for the moment. Mention of "the Crawling Chaos" had triggered a memory—something half-buried, that I had almost contrived to forget, but suddenly had the impression that I ought to strive with all my might to remember....

"I wrote it down," I whispered.

"Wrote what down?" Saint-Germain wanted to know.

"The music...."

"What music?"

"No...not the music, as such...but the story. Something happened...it must have been about three years ago...something important...something so important that I actually wrote it down, although it took me hours on end...."

"To send to your literary friend in America, no doubt?"

"No...not that time. So that...so that...I want to say 'So that I'd remember it' but I have the craziest impression that it was for exactly the opposite reason...so that I'd forget."

"What on earth are you blathering about?" Saint-Germain demanded. "In case you've forgotten, we have urgent business on our hands—not that we'll be able to do anything about that, if this accursed cab remains stuck on this side of the river. There's no point in trying to go home now—we'd best go straight to the Baron's house. Even if he has been working with Tommaso behind my back, he still trusts me...I think. If Tommaso did give him any documents, he'll surely let me see them...."

He began hammering on the partition of the cab again, and when he had attracted the weary coachman's attention, he shouted a new address. Like his own, it was on the left bank, but much further to the east, not far from the Saltpêtrière, where Dupotet had, until recently, been attempting to carry out an ill-fated series of experiments in mesmeric anesthesia.

The coachman twitched his whip symbolically, but it had no immediate effect; for the moment, it seemed, the horse could not move—not that it was in any hurry to try, in all probability. The market traders were beginning to sort themselves out, however, and the carts that had brought in produce from the surrounding area were beginning to retreat again, heading back home to begin the cycle all over again for the following day. I estimated that the roads, and the bridges over the Seine, would become navigable again in less than an hour.

It occurred to me to wonder whether Dupin had decided to walk purely and simply because he had known that he would be able to reach his destination more rapidly than a wheeled vehicle. One of his oft-quoted tenets was that simple explanations were often the most likely, and that it was unwise to be needlessly ingenious. I could not honestly say, however, that his own intellectual conduct routinely did much honor to the principle.

Finally, the fiacre began to move, soon turning left into a narrow and rather noisome alleyway. The interior of the vehicle was plunged into near-darkness again, the burgeoning daylight being reduced to a narrow strip high above its roof.

"At last," Saint-Germain muttered. "I was beginning to think that I had found the only cabman in Paris ignorant of the capital's short cuts."

Alas, his optimism as direly short-lived. The cab suddenly lurched, and came to a stop.

Saint-Germain stuck his head out of the *portière*, to discover what had interrupted our progress, but obviously could not see clearly enough in the narrow and dingy street. He thumped on the partition yet again and shouted, but obtained no reply "See what it is, Donatien," he ordered.

Donatien opened the carriage door and leaned out—and then suddenly collapsed, falling out of the vehicle and into the street. At the same moment, the other door was flung open, and someone reached in to grab me by the lapels of my overcoat.

I could not make out more than a vague blur, but it must have been a strong man, for he dragged me out of the vehicle with a single mighty heave, and slammed me into the wall of the building beside the carriage.

The impact seemed to jar every bone in my body, and it knocked me silly, but I did not smash my head on the brickwork and did not lose consciousness immediately. Indeed, I think that I actually tried to summon some resistance, and for at least half a minute I was let alone while the fiacre's attackers focused their attention on Saint-Germain, but when I actually tried to lash out with my cane—which was not, alas, a swordstick—I only managed to land one feeble blow before I was grabbed from behind and felt the prick of a sharp-pointed blade at my throat.

"Be still, or I'll puncture your windpipe!" hissed a voice with a marked Italian accent.

I believed him, and froze. As my eyes adapted to the darkness I perceived Saint-Germain being dragged away by two other men, and realized that we were hopelessly outnumbered.

For a further half-minute, I hoped, and actually contrived to believe, that it was only Saint-Germain they wanted, and that they would simply let me go once they had him safe—but in that, I was the one who was far too optimistic. I heard someone in the gloom bark an order and although I did not know enough Italian to be certain of its exact meaning, I took the inference that it boded ill for me. Without the pointed dagger relaxing its pressure—which must surely have drawn blood, I thought— something was clamped over my face.

I recognized the scent of the liquid soaking the wad of German tinder immediately, thanks to my recent close acquaintance with the inner sanctums of the Saltpêtrière: it was chloroform.

I knew that the sensible thing to do was to hold my breath, but there are moments in a man's life when panic takes over his flesh, and the rational will simply cannot impose its wise control. Like a fool, I struggled, reflexively—and like a fool, I fell unconscious in a matter of seconds.

CHAPTER SIX
IN THE CATACOMBS

When I recovered consciousness, I had another fit of panic, for I found, long before I opened my eyes, that I was lying on an exceedingly hard stone floor, with my ankles pinned together and my wrists bound behind my back. The floor was as dirty as it was hard, and I could feel vile damp in my clothes; I knew that I must have been there for some time. The floor did not seem unduly cold, but that was no relief; my head was pounding now, and there was sweat on my brow and temples; I would have been grateful for a cool draught, but the air was still motionless and oppressive.

The sensible thing to do would have been to lie perfectly still, pretending unconsciousness until I had had an opportunity to ease my headache and evaluate the situation, but, in the circumstances, I think I can be forgiven for reacting more instinctively. I struggled, thus revealing to anyone who happened to be watching that I would soon be capable of seeing, hearing and speaking.

While I was still trying to lift eyelids that seemed to have been sealed with gum, I was picked up and manhandled into a sitting position. My bones, already jarred more than once, made their protest plain in a surge of pain that made me cry out, inarticulately—although the sound that actually emerged from my throat was more gurgle than scream. I felt a layer of dried blood cracking on my neck, and knew that the point of the stiletto really had penetrated my flesh, somewhere in the vicinity of the jugular vein. The blood-loss must have been trivial, though, else my head could not have been pounding so fervently.

When I eventually did contrive to open my eyes I had to blink them furiously, as much to loosen the stickiness as to adapt my pupils to the light, which came from a single oil-lamp and was far from bright. Indeed, the place in which I found myself seemed so very gloomy and ominous that it would have been a perfect stage-set at the Porte-Saint-Martin for a bandit's cave or a vampire's vault. It seemed to be a large rectangular space opening up at either side into pitch-dark tunnels, the walls of which had been extensively worked by tools of various sorts in the not-very-recent past.

Making the immediate assumption that we could not be in some Corsican grotto or Hungarian vault, I leapt to the conclusion that we were somewhere in the catacombs—or, to give them their more appropriate name, the *carrières*: the underground workings from which primitive masons had quarried the stone that built the city's various walls and many of its most august monuments. Many of the cavities thus opened up had been reclaimed for use as ossuaries when the cemeteries of Old Paris were methodically cleared, and a good deal of supportive masonry-work had been done during the Restoration under the aegis of Héricart de Thury, to such excellent effect that the ossuaries had now been added to the list of attractions offered by the capital to its increasingly-multitudinous tourists. Had this particular excavation been full of bones it might have seemed even more appropriate as a setting, but our captor's sense of melodrama was obviously not as refined as that of our contemporary playwrights. At least its walls had not yet been significantly disfigured by graffiti.

It did not surprise me that Neapolitan bandits—if that was, indeed, who our captor's minions were—knew about the catacombs, for the subterranean passages had long been a favorite refuge for all manner of exiles and criminals.

I had immediately begun to think in terms of "our" captor because the chair on which I had been so rudely arranged was next to another, on which Saint-Germain was sitting, already wide awake and similarly trussed—and I immediately set "captor" in the singular, even though there must have been at least five men present in the capacious space, because only one of them was standing in front of us, in the full glare of the lamplight, and he was very obviously in command.

The others, who were sitting in the shadows, resting and eating a primitive meal, were clad in workmen's blouses, knee-length breeches and clogs. They were obviously hirelings, albeit not of local stock. The man confronting his prisoners with a thin-lipped smile of triumphant determination was quite different in kind, age and status. He wore a frock-coat, full-length trousers, silken stockings and leather boots. His waistcoat was claret in color, and his shirt was as well-bleached as it was well-tailored. Under other circumstances, I might have deemed he and Saint-Germain to be birds of a feather—dandies, that is, in the style that was reputed to have been pioneered by the late Lord Byron, whose reputation in Italy remained even higher than it was in Paris, and far higher than it was in censorious England, where his publisher was said to have burned his memoirs in order to protect the public from offense. The rival dandy was, however, considerably older that Saint-Germain appeared to be—at least seventy, given that his once-black hair was almost all silver now—and retained beneath his dandified exterior a kind of conspicuous hardness suggestive of military training and a life of action. He was holding a substantial dagger—almost a poniard—in his right hand, as if he were well used to playing with such toys.

"Don't let me interrupt," I murmured, when he glanced in my direction—mainly to discover whether I was yet capable of speech. "This is between you and Saint-Germain."

"You are an unnecessary complication," the dandy admitted, with a sigh. He spoke with an Italian accent just pronounced enough to make him seem even more menacing. "I don't approve of complications—especially unnecessary ones."

"Don't be ridiculous," said Saint-Germain. "You've already

got far more complications than you can handle. If, as I assume, you replaced the driver of our fiacre when he went to fetch water from his horse with one of your own men, you must already know that Dupin is at the Prefecture as we speak. They might not have been prepared to take much interest in a dead *bravo* yesterday, but the entire Sûreté will be on the move by now. You can't possibly imagine that *this* is a safe hiding-place, no matter how long it is since you were last in Paris"

It was bluster, and I could tell from his tone that he had no confidence in its likely effect himself—but it had more impact than he had anticipated. The Italian frowned. "What dead *bravo*?" he asked, sharply.

Saint-Germain was taken by surprise, too. "Valdoni," he retorted. "You shouldn't have killed him—it wasn't necessary."

Our captor seemed genuinely nonplussed. "*Carlo* Valdoni?" he queried. "The Venetian adventurer? Carlo Valdoni is dead—and you think *I* killed him?"

St. German had realized his mistake by now, and bit his lip, lest he give away anything more without intending to. When he spoke again, it was to say: "Who are you?"

I didn't suppose that he really expected an answer, and he didn't get one, although his rival dandy did not have sufficient sense of theatrical melodrama to slap him across the face and say: "I ask the questions."

Instead, he said: "You're right, my friend—there are already too many complications in this strange affair. It's time to simplify matters. All that you need to do is to send instructions to your servants to hand over the Guadagnini, and tell us where the girl is, and all the complications will disappear from your life, as they will from mine."

Saint-Germain actually laughed, unable to help himself. "What girl?" he asked, with a note of contempt as well as asperity in his voice. "And what in the Devil's name is a Guadagnini?"

The Italian's gaze abruptly shifted to me, although I was sure that I had given no visible hint that I knew what he was talking about. "Has this clown really contrived to take over the Harmonic Society of Paris?" he asked me. "Has he really convinced them that he's the same Comte de Saint-Germain who tutored Cagliostro? Or is he too clever for his own good—and far too brave?"

I had no time for long consideration as to how to play my part—no time to ask myself *What would Dupin do? Or What would Poe recommend to one of his heroes?* I had to improvise. "You would be wise not to underestimate him," I said to the Italian, trying to sound sure of myself. "Whether he really is the Comte de Saint-Germain, rejuvenated or reincarnated, I cannot say—but he *is* an adept in magnetism and magic, and you toy with him at your peril."

"I know *that*," the other replied, contemptuously. "He has been staring at me since he contrived to open his eyes, hoping to bend me to his will—but I am a truer adept than he is, and not to be bent."

Dupin's opinion was that the eyes, only being windows to the soul in a poetic sense, have no particular power of their own, but that the effort of staring is a psychological device that allows a magnetizer to gather and focus his resources, and that the awareness of being stared *at* can, and usually does, create a real sense of vulnerability, intimidation and capitulation in an intended victim or patient. I assumed that he was probably right—but that had never helped me to resist the force of a magnetizer's stare, and this one was certainly getting the better of me.

"Even so," I said to the self-styled adept, doggedly, "you must know that you are dealing with authentic magic here, and are treading on direly dangerous ground. I don't know whether you are an instigator in this affair, or a mere hireling, but in either case, I warn you that it is no small inconvenience to have the Sûreté combing Paris for you—and to risk releasing the harmonies of hell is something worse. Are you really sure that you want to take possession of the Guadagnini?"

I honestly had not calculated the recklessness of that speech until the Italian's already-intimidating stare sharpened even further. Saint-Germain had a Mesmerist's eyes, and was capable of using them cleverly enough, but this man was at least his equal, as he had claimed, and seemed—at least for the moment—more malevolent by far.

"You think that I'm a hireling?" he said with a mildness more ominous than any anger. "You think that I can be intimidated with threats of magic? You think that I, who have been searching for the Guadagnini for the greater part of my life, would be afraid to set my hands upon it? Do you have the slightest idea who you're talking to?"

I was extremely obliged to him for setting up a line that might diminish the tension. "No," I replied, frankly. "Who?"

Oddly enough, he seemed to see the joke, and almost laughed. "*He* said you were just an innocent fool who had stumbled into the affair, and that I should let you go," he said, flicking a negligent finger in Saint-Germain's direction.

I looked at Saint-Germain, realizing that he had actually tried to help me, and had tried, albeit by belittling me, to persuade his adversary that I was harmless and thus need not be harmed. I made a mental note to be grateful to him for that, if we were fortunate enough to get out of the mess alive. Unfortunately, I seemed to have spoiled his ploy.

"But it does not matter," the dandy continued. "The point is to keep things simple. You, Monsieur le Comte, will simply send a written instruction to your servants, ordering them to surrender the Guadagnini—which, as your friend seems to know, although you pretend not to, is the violoncello that you removed from Grigoryi Mazzoli's house. Then you will tell me where to find the girl—whose name, since you are pretending not to know that as well, is Maddalena. When I have them both safe, I will let you go, and you will never see me again. Until then...I'm afraid that you will be a trifle uncomfortable."

I knew that Saint-Germain's mind had to be working with all possible rapidity, and that he too would be forced to improvise. I had every confidence in his audacity, if not his wise judgment.

"Maddalena is no longer a girl," he said, with a hint of

contempt. "She's an old woman—and whatever witchcraft she once possessed has shriveled with the rest of her. And you're right—it was unpardonably ignorant of me not to realize sooner that Guadagnini must be the name of an Italian luthier, and that the cello must be of his manufacture. As you ought know to know, however, if your substitute coachman was not completely incompetent in his eavesdropping, it is my friend who did not know what an egregore is, and required enlightenment from me."

That was enough to bring the Italian's attention back to Saint-Germain. "Any man might know the meaning of a word," he observed. "To know the creature itself is another matter entirely. If Grigoryi confided any part of his secret to you, you must have honored your commitment to be discreet—but that seems to me to be an ominous sign rather than a matter for congratulation. If you really know nothing, then all this might have been a trifle heavy-handed, but if you have any ambition to employ the cello...."

"Whatever employment I might make of it is none of your business," Saint-Germain stated, flatly. "The instrument belongs to the Harmonic Philosophical Society of Paris. Grigoryi Mazzoli left it to the society in his will, evidently because he thought the Society deserving of it."

"And you think that he was paying your Society a compliment? Well, perhaps he was—but if ever there was a poisoned chalice, the Guadagnini is one. If you know anything at all about the egregore, you must be aware that the cello is a direly dangerous object to possess, let alone to play. I can assure you that you would be wise to surrender it."

I knew that Saint-Germain, like Dupin, was the kind of man who would only become more determined to hold on to the cello once an argument of that sort was put to him. Obviously, he had been right to fear that he might be in danger of harm while he had the cello, and right to ask for Dupin's help in trying to figure out what shape that threat might take—but I did not suppose for a moment that he was going to back out of the affair now, even if he were forced to surrender the object.

"Tell me why," was Saint-Germain's stubborn response to the veiled threat—and I could almost feel the blaze in his eyes, although we were seated in parallel. The fire in his rival mesmerist's eyes I could see, and was grateful that it was no longer directed at me. I could not help feeling, though, that if Saint-Germain had approached the problem more diplomatically, he might have stood a better chance of obtaining an answer to his demand.

"I do not know you," was what the silver-haired man actually said in reply to Saint-Germain's challenge, "and I dare not trust you. I am sure that Grigoryi never confided in any of the other Mesmerists to whom he must tentatively introduced himself through the medium of your semi-secret society during the last forty years, but if he sensed his death approaching, he might well have grown reckless. But all that is irrelevant...simply agree to write the note, and tell me where Maddalena is, and our business will be done."

"We have no idea where Maddalena is," I put in, trying to help, "and if we knew why the cello is so important to you...."

He returned his intimidating gaze to me. "You mentioned the harmonies of hell," he said, as if the significance of the phrase had just occurred to him. "That wasn't just a flowery phrase, was it? You do know something of the cello's potential, and you're playing games with me. What did Grigoryi tell you?"

"Nothing," I told him, glad to be able to be honest. "I never even met the man."

"You, then?" The Neapolitan had turned to Saint-Germain again. "What did he tell *you*?"

"Too little, it seems," Saint-Germain muttered, flexing his arms to test his bonds, which seemed to be holding firm. He might have done better to echo my "nothing", because his interrogator picked up some inference from the tenor of his resentment.

"Who *did* he tell, then?" the silver-haired man was quick to ask. "Come on—*who*?"

Saint-Germain shook his head stubbornly. "How should I know?" he countered. His anger was presumably honest, although his answer was not. "He was a member of the Society for thirty-five years before I joined its ranks. The Marquis de Puységur, probably—they were in collaboration at one time." He knew that it was safe to name a dead man.

The Neapolitan shook his head. "No," he said. "Had he told Puységur, word would have got back to the society in Naples, and...well, suffice it to say that there are people there still who would have been very glad indeed to put him to death. Only the imminence of death would have loosened his tongue. So, I ask you again—if not you, *who*? The Baron Du Potet?" Obviously, his substitute coachman had sharp enough ears to have heard that name spoken, but perhaps not to overhear exactly what was said in that connection.

Saint-Germain was still determined to avoid the question, and obviously thought it best to do so by deflection, now that Dupotet's name had actually been mentioned. "I will admit that I do not know the cello's secret," he said, "and might not care to employ the instrument if I did, given what little I have heard rumored regarding *egregoroi*...but I don't know you, any more than you know me, and I'd be failing in my duty as the President of the Harmonic Society if I did not do everything in my power to safeguard an object possessed of any kind of magical power—for we are scientists, and the reason for the society's existence is to investigate, understand and master such things."

"Master?" the other countered. "Do you think that *you* can master the egregore?"

"Do you?" Saint-Germain countered. "Did Grigoryi?"

The silver-haired man scowled—but the annoyance Saint-Germain had provoked only served to concentrate his mind, even though the tactic of deflection seemed to have succeeded. "Where is Maddalena?" the Neapolitan demanded, in a tone silky with menace.

"I haven't the slightest idea," Saint-Germain retorted. "If I'd known she was important, I'd have made sure that I did, but I was under the impression that she was merely a deaf-mute housekeeper—until I gave her back the power of speech."

That ploy seemed to fail too, although it did prise loose some further information that was not without interest. "Deaf-mute?" the Neapolitan queried. "She was neither deaf nor mute when I knew her. How long has she been unable to sing?"

"How should I know?" Saint-Germain repeated. "She was in Paris for thirty-five years before I first clapped eyes on her.

The silver-haired man did not want to be deflected again. "I'll find Maddalena on my own," he said, as if to himself, "but I need that letter—and I've wasted enough time." He raised his left hand as if to summon one of his companions—but the other bandits were still busy with their meal, and none was looking in his direction. Saint-Germain had shaken off the worst after-effects of the chloroform now though, and was not about to give up on his stubborn quest for enlightenment.

"If I'd known that the cello was so important, of course," he said, "I wouldn't have wasted so much time on the box, but I'm beginning to see the light, now…Monsieur Mazzoli."

If the silver-haired man really was a Mazzoli, he did not answer to his name by any sign that I could see. He did, however, hesitate as he raised his right hand—the one holding the dagger. It was as if he were torn between the intention of freeing Saint-Germain's right hand so that the Mesmerist might write the letter he had demanded, and the possibility that it might be worth the effort of applying a little mild torture, just in case Saint-Germain could give him some clue as to Maddalena's where-abouts, or give him the name of someone to whom Grigoryi Mazzoli might have confided the cello's secret.

"You might want to hurry, Signor Mazzoli," I suggested to him, trying to repay the favor that Saint-Germain had appar-ently tried to do for me.

"I'm not afraid of the Sûreté," he snapped.

"Perhaps not," I replied. "But you're not the only one intent on recovering the cello, are you? If you didn't hire Carlo Valdoni to recover the Guadagnini from Saint-Germain, who did? And if you didn't kill him, who did?"

That shot hit home, more effectively than any other Saint-Germain or I had loosed. "Valdoni was hired to recover the Guadagnini?" the silver-haired man said, his voice rising slightly in pitch, and not only by virtue of the interrogative inflection. "Who told you that?"

"Carlo did," Saint-Germain was quick to put in, "when he came to warn me after refusing the commission—an honorable action that seems to have cost him his life."

Now the Neapolitan was genuinely confused. "Carlo Valdoni refused a commission?" he said, manifestly incredulous, even though he only seemed to know the man by reputation. "And was assassinated in consequence? That's nonsense."

"It's the truth," Saint-Germain told him, insistently. "He owed a greater debt to me than to the code of his profession. In Venice, I once saved the life of his infant son. You may be a mere Neapolitan bandit, but you will understand why he had to refuse a commission to injure me."

I assume that the reference to a "mere Neapolitan bandit" must have stung the silver-haired dandy, but perhaps not as much as the suggestion that he was not the only person hunting for the cello and Maddalena—and that the other, whoever it might be, was already ahead of him in the chase, albeit that he had come up against an unexpected obstacle. The Neapolitan seemed extremely annoyed now—which did not bode well for the likelihood of our eventual release without any harm done, but gave me a certain grim satisfaction nevertheless.

Alas, Dupin was probably deep in the bowels of the Prefecture, carefully sifting through ancient records, languishing in anti-quarian delights! Who, then, was going to save us, if we could not do it ourselves?

"Who hired Valdoni?" the Italian demanded of Saint-Germain, whose face contrived to get even paler than it had been before, as he realized once again that we might both have done better to keep our mouths shut.

"I don't know," the Comte replied, stoutly. "I had assumed that it was you—but you've just told us that there are others interested in your relative's fate. Even if you came from Naples as quickly as humanly possible, there were Italians enough in the capital already. Once news of Tommaso Angelotti's real name had leaked out...."

The silver-haired dandy cursed, in a language that did not seem to me to be pure Italian. Then he jumped to the same conclusion that Saint-Germain had reached, under similar inspiration. In a tone hardly above a whisper, he muttered: "Never trust a lawyer! The only wonder is that it did not happen before Grigoryi died...." He stopped, and raised his dagger again. Mine was not the throat he menaced with it, but I could see by the way it glinted in the lamplight that it had two keen edges. It looked as if it could slice a man's windpipe as easily as a barber's razor. "Fetch that table!" he barked at his idling companions.

This time, they responded immediately. A rickety table was fetched from the shadows, along with an ink-well, a sheaf of quills and several sheets of paper, and the ensemble set beside the chair on which Saint-Germain was uncomfortably perched. The dandy lowered his weapon again and cut the bonds securing the Comte's hands. "Write," he commanded, tersely.

CHAPTER SEVEN
A NECROMANTIC TARANTELLA

Saint-Germain massaged his right wrist with his left hand, trying to restore proper blood circulation, and shrugged his shoulders angrily when his throat was threatened yet again with the dagger's point. The Neapolitan granted him time to recover his flexibility and steadiness of hand, however, and Saint-Germain eventually began to write, a trifle uncomfortably but rapidly.

"It's up to you to make sure that your servants recognize your handwriting and obey your instruction," the Italian told him. "No tricks—simply instruct them to hand over the cello to the note's bearer. If anything goes wrong, and they refuse to surrender the instrument...."

"Whalen is reliable," Saint-Germain assured him, as he laid down the quill. "He'll know what...."

He broke off in mid-sentence, not because of any gesture involving the dagger, but because he had heard something. Indeed, we had all heard something—and I suspect that we were all equally astonished. I could not have been the only one to feel an immediate pang of dread. The Neapolitan cursed one of his followers volubly—presumably the coachman, who had not realized that the stolen fiacre was being followed, any more than I had.

What we heard was music. It was the music of what Saint-Germain would probably have referred to as a "gypsy fiddle"—

not merely because the instrument involved was a violin but because it was playing music of the sort that the wandering players who invaded the capital in the summer favored: hectic and vivid, designed for dancing. The familiarity of style was, however, complemented with a sinister undertone. Little as I knew about the supposed harmonies of hell, I knew by the way the hairs on the back of my neck seemed to stand on edge that this was no paradisal harmony. I had often heard the casual assertion that gypsies routinely played "the Devil's music", but had always dismissed it as abusive hyperbole; on this occasion, though, the charge seemed plausible.

Oddly enough, however, the whine of the violin seemed to soothe my headache rather than aggravating it, as might have been expected. In purely physical terms, I began to feel better.

Had the tune been a little faster and merrier, I might have labeled it, albeit hesitantly, as a jig, for want of any better Anglo-American term. The word that actually sprang to mind, however, was *tarantella*. That word came into my head not because I was familiar with the dance in question or the music that was supposed to accompany it, but because I knew that it was so-called because of its metaphorical association with the bite of a poisonous spider. From the very first chord, I knew— as my companion and captor must have known—that there was something venomous about that tune: something unholy and unwholesome. Although the rhythm was relatively slow, there was something in its sheer insistence that was urgent and ominous. It was as if some sort of itch were running through the muscles of my limbs, as if avid to seize control of them. In purely physical terms, it was not unpleasant...but there was nothing virtuous in its asexual caress.

For a moment or two I was actually glad that my hands and feet were bound, and even that the friction of the cords was gradually becoming agonizing. Agony, I thought, might be the only weapon I had at my disposal to combat the sinister itch and restrain my limbs from a horrid kind of slavery.

The gladness did not last, alas, for two competing horrors

cannot cancel one another out.

At first, I had not the slightest idea which direction the music might be coming from, although I knew that the violin-player must be moving slowly along one of the tunnels to the left or right of the rectangular space—but the uncertainty did not last long. The music grew steadily louder, and more insistent, as the player approached. Paradoxically, the itch in my limbs was supplemented by a kind of creeping paralysis in my limbs, which amplified the paradoxical vexatiousness of the itch by combining a relentless urge to move and twitch with an utter inability to do so, without diminishing the discomfort of the cords binding my wrists and ankles. The momentary gladness was, in consequence, replaced by a subnstantial dose of dread, and I wondered whether Hell could possibly contain a subtle combination of tortures to match it. The worst thing of all was that I knew that no real harm was being done to my flesh, and that the complicated sensation might, therefore, be capable of enduring forever.

As soon as I was sure which direction the sound was coming from, I tried to turn my head, but could not do it. I took what meager comfort I could, however, from the conviction that I was not the only one being inflicted with that infernally tender itch and its concomitant paralysis. Our silver-haired captor was standing still, and perfectly rigid—and so, for the moment, were the two men who had brought the table and writing implements, and the other two still sitting in the shadows.

I could barely see Saint-Germain from the corner of my eye, but I was sure that he was trying to speak, or perhaps to scream. His throat and tongue were frozen, though, and he could not make a sound.

As a lover of music, I had known many kinds of musical effects; I had been roused by music and saddened by music, made exultant and moved to tears—but I had never dreamed that music was capable of worming its way so deeply into my soul: far more deeply than consciousness and perhaps more deeply than the utmost depths of forgetfulness and sleep. I had even experienced magical music before, although I had somehow contrived to repress the memory of it—but this was more intrusive by far than the vibration of the spoiled Stradivarius, for all that it was presumably being produced by a much inferior machine.

In spite of my confusion, the buried memory than I had already begun to recover in the fiacre came flooding back now in fuller measure, and I half-expected to see a diabolical child come marching out of the gallery to my left, carrying some shadowy instrument fuming with infernal smoke. The fiddler who actually appeared in the orifice of the tunnel, however, sawing away at what seemed at first glance to be a perfectly ordinary violin, was an old woman I had never seen before, but whose name I immediately guessed.

This, I knew, must be Maddalena.

She seemed to be *very* old, and *very* ugly. I could understand why Saint-Germain had formed such a low opinion of her that he could not take seriously the possibility that she was behind the execution of Carlo Valdoni—but it was an opinion I could not share, now that I could hear her play the violin. Indeed, it suddenly seemed to me to be absurd that we had considered any other hypothesis, even momentarily, to account for Valdoni's death. She it had to be who had tried to hire the bravo—who had probably formed as contemptuous an opinion of her as Saint-Germain, on the basis of her appearance and speaking voice, and might well have shown that contempt in refusing her commission. She it was who had stabbed the Venetian, probably for that very reason rather than any real anxiety that he might say more to Saint-Germain than he already had.

Dupin was right, as usual; the simplest answer is often the correct one. For once, the lawyer was not to blame.

Thought of Dupin reminded me that he was a confirmed pedant, and there were certain words to which he had a principled objection, although that did not entirely prohibit him from using them. One such word was *supernatural*, because he claimed not only that everything that ever had happened had to be reckoned natural, but that everything that could possibly happen in the future had also to be reckoned natural, and that any violation of apparent possibility had to be reckoned a failure of human understanding and imagination rather than a breach of natural law. Another word that he disliked was "somnambulism", in the meaning attached to it by the Marquis de Puységur, with reference to subjects acting under the influence of Mesmeric authority, or "animal magnetism"—yet another term of which he was not fond. Most Mesmeric "somnambulists," Dupin was fond of pointing out, did not walk at all, but merely talked, for which reason they ought to be called "somniloquists."

I could not help thinking, as the violin-playing Maddalena sidled into our presence in that neglected corner of the boneyard that the *carrières de Paris* had become, that it might have chastened Dupin slightly to see her—for she, with not a shadow of a doubt about it, was a somnambulist and not a somniloquist... and I could not, even with the benefit of all the pedantry in the world, consider her behaviour *natural*.

Dupin might have been pleased as well as chastened, for he was an eager coiner of words as well as a finicky employer of esoteric terminology and I remembered quite clearly now, although I had forgotten it for nearly three years, that he had once made reference to "somnimusicality": the improvisation of music under Mesmeric authority. Maddalena was no mere somnambulist, but a somnimuscian too, for I had no sooner caught sight of her than I felt absolutely certain that she was not playing that violin of her own accord. It seemed infinitely more likely that *it* was playing *her*, as the rogue Stradivarius had played Dupin in the Rue d'Auseuil, at the behest of some otherworldly entity.

This, I felt sure, was my first oblique glimpse of an egregore.

The musician and the instrument, I judged, were both under an immediate and urgent command—so immediate and urgent that a sinister sensation suggested to me that I might even have been able to see the monstrous puppet-master in question lurking in the shadows, watching the scene that was unfolding under its careful direction, if my weak human eyes had only been able to see a little further into the darkness....

The direction *was* careful, and had to be, for it was also very precarious. I had never believed the Comte de Saint-Germain's claim to be a powerful adept in magic rather than a common-or-garden magnetizer with a flamboyant line of patter, and I had doubts about our mysterious captor's similar claim, but my head was turned sideways just far enough for me to be able to glimpse Saint-Germain's face from the corner of my eye, and the Italian was still standing in front of him, more securely in my field of vision. I could see that both of them were trying with all their might to invoke whatever power was latent in their own Mesmeric eyes—but the music was too powerful to be kept at bay.

Perhaps, if they had been able to look at Maddalena directly, they might have succeeded in breaking, or at least weakening, the spell that was upon her, but they could not. As she moved further into the open space, she was careful to remain behind the Italian, and some way to Saint-Germain's left. That meant that she eventually came to a position almost directly in front of me, but she had nothing to fear from my gaze, and seemed to know that.

Indeed, it seemed that I was the one with something to fear, for she looked me directly in the face, and I wished with all my heart that I could lower my frozen eyelids. Although she was remarkably unprepossessing woman, in terms of the shape and slackness of her features, the coarse texture of her skin and the bloodlessness of her shriveled lips, her eyes caught the lamp-light so cleverly as to be radiant with an emotion I took to be wrath.

Had I had a voice, I would have begged for mercy; in the absence of one, I implored mercy from God—and perhaps he heard my prayer, for it suddenly seemed that the pain of the cords binding my limbs loosened its grip. The itch did not go away, nor did the paralysis relax, but the sensation of hideous spiders crawling within my secret self became markedly less disturbing...to the point at which the admitted tenderness of the itch became genuinely soothing, authentically comforting. I felt as if my consciousness were bathing is some kind of balm, its affliction by pain and horror alike diminishing in consequence.

Then Maddalena looked away. Apparently, I was not the one she had come here to find; in her estimation, as in mine, I was presumably just a bystander, and harmless. She did not move any closer to Saint-Germain or his persecutor, but she did redirect her attention toward one or both of them. They were still standing perfectly still, but I felt sure that there was a genuine contest going on, in which the two erstwhile rivals now found themselves united against a common foe. The violin-player had the upper hand in the contest of wills, by virtue of her music, but the instrument's mastery was by no means unchallenged.

Over the Italian's common-or-garden bandits, however, the music had more control: control enough to make them move by controlling their paralysis, so that they too became somnabulists of a sort, as jerky as marionettes operated by an unpractised puppeteer.

I say that the music had control, rather than attributing that control to Maddalena, because I was perfectly sure that it was not *her* will that was commanding the obedient minions. It really was the music: that bizarre tarantella, which somehow contrived to be fluid and staccato at the same time, and so replete with awful darkness that it made a mockery of the right of any milder and more sentimental piece to the name of *nocturne*. That might have been a distinction without a difference, had she been the one remembering or improvising the music, but I could not believe that she was. That impossibility of belief was not because she was an old woman, but because of something in the music itself: an independence and an unconstrained authority.

Unconstrained—but by no means omnipotent.

At first, the tarantella attempted to command all of the brigands, causing all four to move in eerie unison, like members of a crazy chorus line, but that was probably an error of judgment on the puppet-master's part. After a minute or two, all save one of them froze into immobility; that one became the tarantella's only active slave...apart from the player herself.

The one active man moved toward the statue in the frock-coat, with evidently menacing intent.

I was convinced at the time, and still believe, that what the "dancer" was supposed to do was to take the dagger from his erstwhile master's hand and plunge it into his heart, and then, quite probably, to plunge it into Saint-Germain's breast too—but not, I felt sure, into mine. It seemed, however, that the first part of that commission was proving direly difficult to accomplish. Maddalena was able to stay well clear of the Neapolitan's line of sight, but the music's second slave was not, and when he reached out to take the dagger he was compelled to hesitate, and to tremble.

For a little while, I thought that the puppet would collapse, but in the end he did contrive to grip the dagger, and to extract it from the Neapolitan's grip. The very fact of his taking possession of it, however, seemed to decrease the authority of the music and increase the power of the silver-haired man's gaze.

The puppet actually took a step away from his intended victim, and turned in the direction of the violin-player, almost as if the dagger had a power akin to the instrument, and intended to use its slavish wielder as a means of murder.

That was when Maddalena began to sing—or *tried* to sing.

According to Saint-Germain, she had recovered the use of her voice sufficiently to rail at him and curse him when he had placed his hand upon her head and tried to calm what he assumed to be hysteria. I wondered now whether it might simply have been the stress of seeing the cello and the box unexpectedly removed from the room where they had rested for half a century that had broken through whatever psychological barrier that had quieted her tongue. In either case, though, she had not recovered her voice sufficiently to make herself fully understood to Saint-Germain, let alone to sing in harmony with the violin. Her voice was still confused, and whether the fault was in her ear or her brain, she could not modulate it properly.

I cannot say for sure that the song she was attempting to sing actually had words—if it had, they were certainly not French or Italian—but I can guarantee that the sequence of wordless squeaks and screeches that she actually emitted was incorrect. That was obvious in the agony of her face as well as the cacophony of the combined sound. Indeed, the attempted song seemed to undermine the command of the tarantella rather than reinforce it.

Maddalena still had power enough to stop the dancer with the dagger advancing toward her, but not enough to make him turn on the figure in the frock-coat. Momentarily, there was a stalemate. Then the player gave up; the song died, and the dagger fell to the floor with a clatter, ending up an inch or two from St, German's bound feet.

I felt the pain of that clatter ripple through me, disturbing the music. I felt, behind that partial interruption, both the awesome power of the egregore and its terrible fragility...or perhaps *brittleness* would be a better word. Like a diamond, there was a sense, at least in terms of poetic analogy, in which the egregore was both extremely hard and extremely delicate, able to drill into substances that steel could not scar, but likely to shatter if abruptly struck in just the right way.

The clatter was not up to that task, though; the egregore played on, as determined as it was desperate. It wanted to kill us all, to clear us out of the way...but it did not have instruments adequate to the task. Maddalena was not adequate, and neither was her violin. This hasty improvisation was costing the egregore dear, for what might yet turn out to be a very poor reward

Once it had dropped the dagger and abandoned its attempt to stab the Neapolitan, however, the puppet seemed to take on a new lease of life. Having turned away from the magnetizer's furious gaze, it took two jerky steps toward the table where the ink and paper lay, and snatched up the piece of paper on which Saint-Germain had written the letter instructing his butler to surrender the Guadagninni cello to its bearer. Then the puppet ran—and I do mean *ran*, although his gait was the strangest human gallop I had ever observed—into the darkness to my left. A few seconds later, I heard him fall, some distance away along the dark tunnel.

The concert wasn't over yet. The music began to build to a kind of crescendo, and the player's human—or semi-human—voice came into play again, no longer attempting to form a song but merely to frame a ear-splitting single note in accompaniment with the violin. Except that it was not a single note at all, but merely the prelude to a gliding change of pitch, without any discernible intervals: a *glissando*, as Dupin had called it, or a *portamento*. I remembered what Dupin had said about harmonic destabilization, and transgression of the relationship between being and time.

The *glissando*, I knew, was another murder attempt—or perhaps an attempt at something more sinister.

I dread to think what might have happened to Saint-Germain and the Neapolitan had the voice been capable of harmonizing with the violin as the player's fingers slid along the instrument's neck, although I still felt strangely sure that I would not have been harmed. At any rate, the capability was lacking, and the resultant combination was a hideous discord. I had thought the preparatory effect ear-splitting, but the *glissando* itself was mind-splitting, or perhaps reality-splitting. It cut through me more trenchantly than any mere dagger, although I did not find the sensation particularly unpleasant. Indeed, I almost felt strong enough to laugh at it, and at all the other petty afflictions still irritating my impatient flesh.

Space, Dupin had assured me more than once, is not really empty; indeed, it is completely full. Not merely is the void between the stars full of universes made of exotic matter, inapprehensible by our feeble senses, but the void within the atoms making up our own tenuous matter is likewise full. There are billions of universes within us as well as without, carefully separated by the mathematical and musical laws that determine their stability and their harmony, and nothing, in Dupin's opinion, can ever happen that is without those laws—nothing truly "supernatural"—although that does not mean that there cannot sometimes be friction between universes, or exchanges across their boundaries. Such exchanges can transfigure or destroy people…and such friction can *hurt*. That agony alone could take all the strength out of a man and render him help- less, Dupin had warned me. Agony caused by that kind of fric- tion could make its sufferer feel emptied out and torn apart; it did not render its victim unconscious, but anyone who had ever been through the experience—and Dupin spoke as someone who had—would affirm that it might be better by far if it did.

Forewarned as I was, that was my expectation when the terminus of the glissando pointed me in the direction of infinity—but it did not quite work out that way.

I saw, from the corner of my eye, that Saint-Germain and the Italian felt the anticipated agony in no uncertain terms. They collapsed, and I felt free to doubt that they would ever get up again—but they had been targeted, and I, it seemed, had not. I felt the surge, but in a strangely indifferent fashion, hardly painful at all. I still felt strong—well-nigh invulnerable, in fact—and when the paralysis that had been holding me rigid released its grip entirely, I merely rearranged my sitting posture so that it was as comfortable as I could make it.

Then—quite naturally, or so it seemed—I simply fell asleep.

CHAPTER EIGHT
A HOPELESS CHASE

I have no idea how much time passed before I woke up again, but I knew even then that it was not a matter of mere minutes, and suspected that it might be as much as several hours. Tightly bound as I was, however, I could not consult my watch. I had to wait for one of the other six men to come round, if any of them were going to recover.

I hoped, of course, that Saint-Germain would regain consciousness first—and he did, although his awakening seemed a great deal less comfortable than my own. In spite of his evident discomfort and a volley of muttered complaints, however, the Mesmerist retained sufficient presence of mind to move as quickly as he could, with his feet still bound, to seize the dagger that was lying on the ground, and then to cut my bonds to free my arms and hands. Then he freed his own feet and moved, as swiftly as he could, to hold it to the Neapolitan's throat.

His bloodshot eyes flickered from side to side, while he prepared to make threats to any of the hirelings who might rise to his feet, but none of them moved. I went to the nearest one and knelt beside him in order to check for a pulse or any sign of breathing. There was none. I investigated the other two in their turn. Both were still alive, mercifully, but deeply unconscious.

Saint-Germain's precaution seemed needless even with respect to our abductor, since the silver-haired man seemed quite unable to rise to his feet, and was barely managing to prop himself up on his elbow. Silence had descended upon the catacombs again; Maddalena had vanished, along with the violin and Saint-Germain's note.

I finally took out my watch and checked the time. It was past noon, but I had no idea what time it had been when I had woken up from the effects of the chloroform, so I couldn't be sure how long the old woman had been gone. Long enough, I suspected.

The silence didn't last long; I dare say that I would have broken it myself within a matter of seconds, but the erstwhile master of the situation got in first, and his groan was exceedingly heartfelt even before it dissolved into near-coherent speech. What he actually said, when the words formed themselves, perhaps independently of any conscious intention, was: "Maddalena! What has he done to you?"

Given his admission that he had not seen Maddalena for more than forty years, I thought that it would have been rather foolish of him to have assumed that time might have treated her any less unkindly than it had, so I assumed that he was referring to the fact that she had apparently been reduced to the status of a marionette: a marionette who, perhaps fortunately, no longer had the voice to accomplish what would surely have been the direr part of her commission.

"It's my turn now to ask the questions," Saint-Germain said to his erstwhile captor, in a manner suggestive of his willingness to use the knife if those questions went unanswered. "*Who are you?*"

"Paolo Mazzoli," the other replied. "Grigoryi's younger brother, albeit by a decade and more—and his legitimate heir." That answer was given in a dispirited tone, but now that he was free of the binding spell of the violin and its deadly tarantella, the man in the frock-coat seemed to rally, and to pull himself together with remarkable rapidity. If, as his answer suggested, he was nearer eighty than seventy, he was in remarkably good condition, as befit an authentic adept in magic.

The effort that Palolo Mazzoli made was visible, but it was also visibly effective. He made no immediate attempt to stand, but he did sit up and stiffen his back. When Saint-Germain moved the dagger toward his throat again he looked up at his rival dandy, with a sneer on his lips that did not seem entirely warranted, given that they were both dishevelled from their fall on to dirty ground.

"Do you really believe that you can stab me with that, any more than the marionette was able to do?" Mazzoli demanded. He was looking Saint-Germain directly in the eyes—but Saint-Germain did not flinch.

"Yes I do," said the President of the Harmonic Philosophical Society of Paris, "I might have doubted it yesterday, but not now. You cannot hold me with your gaze. I have had a revelation, you see. Somewhere in the depths of my soul, I always know that I was not an impostor...but now I know for sure. I really am the Comte de Saint-Germain. I really am."

Strangely, the Neapolitan did not try to contradict that remarkable assertion. Instead, he sighed. "After seeing that," he said, "I could almost believe it."

"She was not playing of her own accord," Saint-Germain stated. "Who is her master? The egregore?"

"Obviously," Mazzoli replied. "It has emerged from hiding—which means that its scheme must be almost complete...but it needs a player for the cello, if it is to increase its power—which it must need to do very desperately, after that botched performance. I ask you again: who will play on its behalf?"

Saint-Germain was not about to submit to interrogation now that he held the dagger. "I'll find out," he said, through gritted teeth. "But if you know so much more than I do, tell me exactly what it is that was guiding your once-pretty lover just now!"

The use of the term *lover* was an obvious provocation, and it worked. "How should I know exactly what form its self-possession takes?" Paolo Mazzoli spat at his interlocutor. "Grigoryi? Cagliostro? Pezza? How can I tell? The *egregoroi* can take on the forms of the dead as well as the living, when they have power enough to draw upon...but this one needs more, and for that it needs players as well as the cello. You're the one who's been acquainted with Grigoryi these last five years. If anyone can identify his living accomplice…."

Saint-Germain had evidently been taken aback by the Neapolitan's wild guesses regarding the forms that the egregore might adopt, although the list seemed like patent nonsense to me. "Cagliostro?" he queried. "You think Cagliostro might have something to do with this?"

"Ask your friend!" the other retorted, venomously. "He's the one who mentioned *Les Harmonies de l'enfer*, which that fool Balsamo had printed—but no…if the egregore were going to reanimate any dead man as a surrogate, it surely wouldn't be Balsamo. It would be Grigoryi…or Pezza. The Devil likely had far more work for *him* to do than he'd so far accomplished."

Saint-Germain might simply have been too proud to ask his adversary who "Pezza" might be, but he probably felt that he had a more urgent mission to complete, and did not want to waste time. At any rate, he turned to me, and said: "We need to get to my house before Whalen hands over that cello, if we can. Then we have to find Dupin, and quickly—if only to tell him that he's a skeptical fool, and that everything he's always denied is true after all. Mesmerism *is* the key to ancient magic, and the mages of old did have secret knowledge that was long since hidden away. Come on! This way!"

I was a little slow to react, because I had a nagging suspicion that I head heard the name Pezza before, and ought to know what its significance was. I frowned, and tried to dip into my memory.

"Pull yourself together, man!" Saint-Germain said. "You weren't the one she was trying to kill—*come on!*"

I followed him, of course, even though I had no faith in the fact that he knew where he was going, or that there was any point in giving chase to a quarry that had surely escaped us. I had no alternative—he had snatched up the lantern as he made his intemperate getaway. Paolo Mazzoli made no attempt to stop him—perhaps because Saint-Germain was running in the same direction that Maddalena had taken, and the Neapolitan feared that something terrible might happen were we to catch up with her. Neither of them, apparently, had yet realized the true extent of the advantage she had gained.

As I started to run after Saint-Germain, however, I could not help feeling an impulse to pedantry myself. Dupin was, in fact, a *true* skeptic, who rarely denied anything and kept an open mind about everything, reserving judgment on all matters when there was no conclusive proof to focus a conclusion. Having witnessed the power of music over the human mind before, as well as its apparent ability to distort the boundaries between universes, he would have had no particular cause for surprise in what we had just witnessed—but nor would he have taken Saint-Germain's suddenly-acquired conviction as solid evidence of the fact that he really was, in some sense, the person he had always pretended to be.

Pedantry was, however, merely a matter of punctuation. The real questions I wanted to pose to myself were concerned with what might happen next, if it transpired—as it almost inevitably would—that we would be too late to prevent Whalen handing over the cello to Maddalena, or her new master. What might Grigoryi, or the mysterious Pezza, or the Baron Du Potet, or someone else entirely, intend to do with the instrument, and how? Was he, she or it intent on carrying out some exotic act of psychic vampirism, or did the ambition in question extend beyond that to something more ingenious? There were, it seemed, far too many possible meanings attributable to the word *egregore* for me to draw any firm conclusion as yet…although I felt unusually confident in my ability to work it out eventually, with or without Dupin's help.

In the tunnel, we found another body—that of Maddalena's principal puppet. Saint-Germain simply jumped over the obstruction, but I paused to check the man's condition. He was dead. Counting Carlo Valdoni, Maddalena and her master now seemed to have been responsible for at least three murders, and had certainly attempted at least two more. I did not, however, have the slightest hesitation in following Saint-Germain when he called on me to hurry. I was committed now, and I was utterly determined to see the business through to its conclusion…whatever strange conclusion that might be.

Whether he knew his way or not, Saint-Germain found a way out of the catacombs readily enough, once he had stumbled into the network of ossuaries where the bones of the ancient Parisian dead were being patiently accumulated and organized. He had evidently been there before—which was not surprising, given scholarly interests and his turn of mind—and once he had got his bearings he moved unerringly to the spiral staircase that led up to the Rue des Catacombes, not far from the Barrière de l'Enfer.

We found a fiacre readily enough, although the coachman looked uneasily at our filthy clothing, and might have refused to let us into his none-too-clean cab had not Saint-Germain thrown him a five-franc piece and threatened him with his intimidating gaze. The nag set off willingly enough, and we headed northwards into the city at a god trot, in spite of the interminable procession of carts that was still headed in the opposite direction. Once we drew closer to the heart of the city, however, we ran into difficulties.

In terms of its sheer volume, the traffic was by no means as bad as it had been first thing in the morning, when we had had all the unloading of the farmers' carts to contend with, but even in somnolent August, the everyday business of finance, commerce, administration and the law never comes to a halt in Paris, and there were plenty of carriages cluttering the streets south of the Île de la Cité, with more than the usual quota of breakdowns and accidents—many of which seemed to have taken place along our route.

Perhaps we were unlucky, or perhaps the mysterious person whose trail we were following had somehow taken precautions, but the simple fact is that we were continually frustrated in our attempt to get back to the Faubourg Saint-Germain in a hurry. In all probability, we would have failed to catch up with Maddalena even if we had had the clearest run imaginable, but as things were, it was obvious long before we reached Saint-Germain's house that we would be too late by far.

When we got there, the cello was long gone—although the box was still safe in the upstairs room, and still emitted the same muffled *clunk* when it was agitated.

Saint-Germain had to restrain himself from scolding Whalen, although he knew that he had no possible grounds for doing so. There were more important questions to ask. Alas, Whalen had not seen anyone but the woman who had brought the note: an old woman, remarkably ugly, who did not seem able to speak or to understand French. She had taken the cello away in a fiacre—without, of course, having said a word to the coachman.

"Did you recognize the coachman, by any chance?" I asked the butler, thinking that the fiacre might be one of those that regularly plied its trade in the neighbourhood.

Whalen shook his head, sadly, evidently disappointed by the fact that obeying his master's orders to the letter had, for once, led to disaster. He picked up a silver tray from the hall table, which contained the morning post carefully arranged in a fan-like array, and offered it to his master as if by way of compensation—but Saint-Germain did not even glance at the letters, simply waving the tray and the crestfallen butler away. The false Comte ran upstairs then, as if some faint hope might remain that the cello would be there after all.

It was not.

"You know," Saint-Germain said to me, as we stood on the threshold of the upstairs room, looking at the empty space where the cello had stood, "I think I might indeed have been slightly mistaken about the reason for Maddalena's over-excitement when I took away the more valuable and interesting items of my inheritance. I'm still convinced that she was cursing me, but I suspect that she might also have been trying to tell me that *she* had been cursed—and that what was in the box was something she needed to defend herself, against the *egregoroi*."

"I suppose you might be right," I said, absent-mindedly, as I moved ahead of him into the room, "but it's pure conjecture."

"I'm a magician," he reminded me. "My conjectures are often inspired." Coming from a man who was now firmly convinced that he really was, in some strange sense, the Comte de Saint-Germain who had allegedly visited Paris in the days of the *ancien régime*, the assertion rang distinctly hollow.

I walked over to the box. I knelt down beside it, and began running the fingers of both hands over the carved foliage. Then, pressing with four fingers simultaneously, in a very particular formation, I contrived to generate a dull click. Then I checked the lid, to make sure that I could lift it freely—but before doing so, I looked up at Saint-Germain, triumphantly.

"How in God's name did you do that?" he demanded, peevishly. "I tried for hours…."

"I don't know," I told him. "It simply felt right."

"Well, don't keep me in suspense," he said. "Lift the infernal lid, and let's see what's inside.

I lifted the probably-uninfernal lid, and looked down into the well of the box. The object within was wrapped in a piece of amber-colored cloth, which I had to unwind. When I had done so, the cloth disgorged a severed human hand. The flesh had withered, so that there was little left but bone covered with leathery skin, but it was definitely the callused and scarred left hand of a man whose life had not been swathed in metaphorical velvet.

As I reached out to grip it—using my own left hand because the right was holding up the lid of the box—it twisted, and gripped my hand in a firm but friendly handshake, which was sinister in more than one sense. I didn't make a sound, but merely looked up again when the grip relaxed and the hand became inert again, wondering what Saint-Germain would have to say to *that*.

He did not say anything; indeed, he did not seem to have noticed anything more untoward than the hand's mere presence in the protective case.

"Is this the kind of talisman that might ward off hostile magic?" I asked him, a trifle hoarsely.

"Some might think so," he admitted, cautiously. "Whose hand do you suppose it is?"

"Tommaso Angelotti's?" I suggested.

"No—he had two when he was laid out in the Morgue."

"Paolo Mazzoli never even mentioned the box," I said, pensively. "Nor did he react when you mentioned it. Maddalena might well have wanted it, but your note didn't give her the authority to demand it, and for the time being, at least, she was prepared to settle for the cello. Unless she intends to come back for it…."

"She still wanted me dead a little while ago," Saint-Germain reminded me, "and Mazzoli too…I suspect it was a close-run thing. She's certainly gained in power since she tried to curse me, and since she tried to hire Carlo. She wasn't in the egrego-re's possession then—not entirely, at any rate—but she is now. Be glad that she didn't attack you as fiercely as she attacked Paolo Mazzoli, else you'd surely not have survived."

"Yes," I said, lifting the hand up so that I could study it more closely. "I was lucky, I suppose."

"That's mine," the President of the Harmonic Society said, staring at the severed hand. "Tommaso left it to me in his will. Dupin can't have it. Give it to me."

I handed it over without a word of protest, placing it in the palm of his extended right hand. "On the Society's behalf, of course," I said, mildly. "Make sure you look after it."

He had the grace to laugh, albeit a trifle sardonically.

CHAPTER NINE
WHAT DUPIN LEARNED
AT THE PREFECTURE

I would have walked home then, in order to clean myself up and change my clothes—both of which operations seemed to have become urgent now that the unnecessarily hectic chase was over and the race accepted as lost, but before I could even broach the subject with Saint-Germain, Dupin was shown into the upstairs room by Whalen. He seemed more than a trifle annoyed to discover that the cello was gone, and looked at me as if I had failed him—although his expression became more sympathetic when I told him, triumphantly, that I had solved the puzzle of the box, and pointed at the severed hand that Saint-Germain was still clutching in his own.

"Well done, my friend," said the great logician, beaten for once to the solution of a puzzle. "Now, all that remains is for us to figure out the hand's significance."

"That's just the merest part of what we've discovered," I told him, a trifle nettled by the modesty of his congratulation. "We have had an extremely eventful day."

"Did you ascertain the identity of the Society member to whom Angelotti might have confided his secrets? *Is* it Dupotet?"

"We never got as far as the Baron's house, alas," I said, still speaking rather stiffly. "We have spent some time in the company of Paolo Mazzoli, however, and encountered the mercurial Maddalena…and, I believe, the egregore itself"

"Really?" he said, as if none of those circumstances was an occasion for surprise. "Who has the cello now?"

Rather than answering him simply and directly, I rapidly recounted the whole story of what had happened since we parted company, sticking to the facts rather than cluttering up the narrative with an account of my unsteady sensations.

"That's most unfortunate," Dupin said, when I concluded by explaining that Maddalena had collected the cello, and had vanished into the sultry afternoon heat. "And exceedingly strange."

Saint-Germain had apparently changed his mind about making much of his supposed opportunity to confound Dupin's alleged skepticism. "What did you discover at the Prefecture, Monsieur Dupin?" he demanded, unceremoniously but politely. "Have you any idea why the cello is so important? And why, if it is so important, has it apparently been sitting quietly in Tommaso Angelotti's house for forty years?"

"Forty years is indeed the interval involved," Dupin confirmed. "Grigoryi Mazzoli had spent some time in Paris prior to that—prior to the Revolution, in fact—but I doubt that he brought the cello with him. He did not become Tommaso Angelotti until 1806, when the emperor's political police—who were then under the direction of the infamous Joseph Fouché—established that identity for him, in order to protect him. The emperor, undoubtedly at Fouché's instigation, awarded him a pension to compensate him, albeit meagerly, for his inability to collect the income on his Neapolitan and Corsican estates."

"So he *was* a spy?"

"No—but he was a traitor...and had his whereabouts been discovered, he would certainly have paid the ultimate penalty for his treason, for the man he betrayed was Michele Pezza."

I suddenly remembered where I had heard that name before. "The bandit!" I said. "Fra Diavolo!" I had seen the opera *Fra Diavolo*, with music by Daniel Auber and a libretto by Eugène Scribe, soon after arriving in Paris, during its first revival at the Opéra-Comique.

"Fra Diavolo indeed," Saint-Germain observed, "if Paolo Mazzoli was correct in thinking that he might have come back from the dead to reclaim the cello—but Mazzoli might not have meant that seriously, and certainly does not seem to have expected any such eventuality. If Maddalena's strings were being pulled by someone else, it's unlikely to have been the ghost of Michele Pezza."

"Maddalena must have been very frightened when you saw her at Grigoryi's house, Saint-Germain," Dupin observed, his brow furrowed—as it always was when he was deep in thought. "If, as you say, she is now a puppet in someone else's hands, and she had any inkling of what might be about to happen to her...."

"Yes," Saint-Germain agreed. "I suppose she was frightened. That, as much as her wrath, is probably why she was ranting about the evil eye and *egregoroi* when I took the cello. She was cursing me with all the venom she could muster—but she might also have been trying to warn me that the cello was direly dangerous. She was afraid of the egregore...the kind of egregore, I assume, that feeds vampirically on the psychic energy of others. And she was right to be afraid."

"That's quite possible," Dupin said, mildly. "Do either of you, perchance, have any idea where we might find Paolo Mazzoli now? It would be useful, I think, if we were able to compare notes with him—and he might be willing to do that, since his own plans have gone awry."

"No," I admitted. "We might, I suppose, have attempted to bring him along with us—and he might have been eager to come, given that he was so enthusiastic to acquire the cello himself—but Saint-Germain was in too much of a hurry."

Dupin sighed. "No matter," he said. "Now that his own plans have misfired and he's in dire danger himself, he'll probably take the trouble to find us."

"About this bandit...." Saint-Germain began.

"My friend's view of Fra Diavolo has been formed at the Opéra-Comique," Dupon cut in, "but Opera houses are not the right place to study history, nor Monsieur Scribe the best person to interpret it. The French have always done their best to diminish and demonize Michele Pezza, but the truth is that he was a soldier, not a bandit—and a highly effective one. He was drawn into the resistance against the French occupation of Naples while enlisted in the Regimento di Messapi in 1798—but when the regular forces were defeated in battle by the Republican Army he took to the hills, and began to fight a very different kind of campaign. The French called it banditry, but from the Neapolitan viewpoint, it was justified patriotic warfare.

"The French set up the puppet Parthenopean Republic to rule Naples, but Pezza and Cardinal Ruffo contrived to overthrow it and liberate their homeland...until the resurgent Empire undertook its reconquest. Pezza had retired with the rank of Colonel, but he immediately returned to active service, and resumed the war of attrition that he had fought before...and might have won again, had the British not removed their support in favour of allies they thought more easily defensible. Pezza fled to Sicily for a while, but returned to fight yet again...and might have been a painful thorn in Napoleon's side until the Empire fell, had he not been betrayed, captured by Joseph Hugo and hanged."

"And Grigoryi Mazzoli was the one who betrayed him?"

"Having previously been one of his most trusted supporters... along with his younger brother Paolo, who remained loyal to the Neapolitan cause, and continued the fight...with the result that he was a hunted outlaw for many years, until the last remnants of Bonapartist rule fell apart.

"The documents relating to Mazzoli's...resettlement...still exist, although it required an expert Archivist to locate them. Fortunately, there is still one man working in the bowels of the Prefecture who was there in 1806, and has a true love of his craft. I was, therefore, not only able to ascertain the facts of the matter, but also to insect some of the copious reports submitted by spies in Naples, relating to Pezza and the Mazzoli family. They must have seemed bizarre at the time, and I doubt that Monsieur Fouché took the slightest notice of their stranger features…but if the Opéra-Comique's hacks had had access to them, their contemporary celebration of the romance of banditry and gypsy witchcraft might have been even more melodramatic than it is."

"Don't tease us, Dupin," said Saint-Germain. "Just tell us what you found."

"The blackening of Pezza's name by his French enemies did not stop with the assertion that he was a mere bandit," Dupin said. "Supportive assertions were also made—quite calculatedly, in accordance with Fouché's strategy—that he was low-born, and had acquired the nickname Fra Diavolo because of a penchant for cruelty cultivated in childhood. In Naples, it seems, a counter-rumor was put around that he had indeed acquired the nickname in childhood, but as an affectionate joke. This seems, however, to be one of those cases when the most obvious answer is the correct one. Pezza was actually nicknamed Fra Diavolo because he really did make a pact with the Devil…ceremonially, at least."

"What's *ceremonially* supposed to mean?" Saint-Germain queried.

"Exactly what it says: he staged a ceremony. As I said, Pezza was not low-born, but came from a good family He was well-educated, in music as well as Latin and Greek."

"He played the cello?" I guessed.

"No—the piano. How accomplished he became, I have no idea—but he was familiar with the instrument and with music written for it. More importantly, however, he also seems to have conceived a fascination for the folk music of the region, much of which was routinely played on the violin. Monsieur de Saint-Germain seems to think of all such music as the work of *gypsy fiddlers*, but the overindulgent use of the word *gypsy* as a term of abuse obscures some very real and very important differences between contrasted populations, some of whom are nomads but many of whom are settled populations living in rural areas relatively undisturbed, thus far, by the relentless march of civilization."

"Including the hills of the kingdom of Naples," I put in, trying to hurry him along. "The region to which Pezza retreated in order to fight his…war of attrition."

"Just so. People who did not consider themselves to be affiliated to any such kingdom; people who, for the most part, did not even speak the same language as the citizens of Naples…and had probably had exactly the same attitude to the Macedonian and Roman Empires two millennia before. Pezza was desperate to acquire their support, not merely in sheltering and feeding his troops, but also in fighting for him…and in order to do that, he needed to make a very special alliance."

"By exploiting their superstitions," Saint-Germain said. "I can understand that."

"Of course you can," Dupin agreed, with a wry smile. "By contrast with the utterly civilized and carefully intellectualized faiths that rub shoulders in the corridors of the Harmonic Philosophical Society of Paris, though, the religion of the people with whom Pezza made alliance was a curious synthesis of ideas forged in the crucible of continual harassment and persecution of Roman Catholicism—a bundle of beliefs so long condemned by the civilized as heretical and Satanic that their adherents had eventually become proud of addressing their worship to the Christian Devil…or, at least, in proclaiming that challenge to outsiders.

"In order to make a pact with them, they required Pezza and his trusted lieutenants to make a formal pact with the Devil. It was probably a test of his sincerity, which he duly passed, and thus became, in name and presumed entitlement, Fra Diavolo. That was a name and a reputation that did him no harm at all as a leader of irregular forces and a claimant of assistance from the people among whom he was now living…most of whom, to tell the truth, probably made no distinction between French oppressors and citizens of Naples, saved for the fact that—for the time being, at least—it was mostly French troops who were marching arrogantly into their homeland, raping, pillaging and killing. If Pezza subsequently acquired a reputation for cruel ill-treatment of his adversaries, it was no less than the one they had acquired for themselves. In that kind of war, both parties tend to have the Devil in their ranks, insofar as their propensity for violence is concerned."

"And Grigoryi Mazzoli was party to this ceremonial pact?" I said, still trying to hurry the story along.

"He was—and his brother too. What words were used to seal the pact I do not know…but the spies who were inevitably present at the ceremony did take the trouble to report on the music played during the ceremony and thereafter."

"Surely not on the piano?"

"On violins and drums, for the most part—with one unusual exception. Grigoryi Mazzoli, who had been educated in much the same spirit as Michele Pezza, was the proud possessor of a cello—and not just any cello, but a cello made in Turin by one of the finest luthiers of the eighteenth century: Giovanni Guadagnini. It was an instrument of recent provenance, made in the 1780s, so it did not have anything like the *cachet* attached to instruments made by Niccolo Amati in Cremona a century before, or by Amati's pupils Guarneri and Stradivarius, but there is superstition in musical history as in every other—and there is also progress in musical history, as in any other. The Gaudagnini cello was a very fine instrument indeed, and the hill folk recognized that, because their lack of formal education did not prevent the musicians among them from having sensitive ears and a highly sophisticated appreciation of the effects that music can achieve…an appreciation that is perhaps more sophisticated, in some respects, than that of civilized ears and minds, and is certainly different in some important respects.

"To what extent Pezza and Mazzoli played on their own knowledge of the hill folk's musical sensibilities in making their treaty, I cannot tell—but even the reports sent back to Paris by ignorant spies emphasize the symbolic importance credited by the parties to the treaty to Grigoryi Mazzoli's cello, to which the credit was given for the manifestation of the Devil to seal the pact. There is a sense in which Fouché's provision of protective asylum for Grigoryi was also a provision of protective asylum for the instrument, which had acquired a talismanic significance by virtue of its role in the rite of conjuration. You can understand, I think, how musical instruments can acquire that kind of significance."

"Drake's drum," I murmured.

"The lost trumpet of Jericho," was Saint-Germain's more esoteric suggestion.

"So Mazzoli's betrayal cut even deeper than it might otherwise have done," I said, hurrying along yet again, "because he took away an important element of the treaty made between Pezza and the hill folk."

"Indeed," Dupin confirmed. "And even deeper than that, when one figures in the personal element."

This time, Saint-Germain and I replied in chorus: "Maddalena."

"Exactly. It was Michele Pezza that Grigoryi turned over to Hugo's troops to be hanged, but he betrayed his brother too—not fatally, but I doubt that his brother appreciated that mercy."

"But that's the stuff of common melodrama!" Saint-Germain put in, with a hint of contempt. "Two respectable brothers in love with the same wild gypsy girl…you can see that any night of the week, in half of the cheap theaters in the Boulevard du Temple…often with a healthy dose of witchcraft thrown in for good measure."

"I'll take your word for that," Dupin said. "Except that Grigoryi Mazzoli was not in love with Maddalena, who was not, strictly speaking, a gypsy, and that the dose of what you call witchcraft that was thrown into this particular melting pot was anything but healthy."

"If he wasn't in love with her, why did he run away with her?" I asked—with a hint of naivety that Saint-Germain was quick to correct.

"You mean," he said, dryly, "if he wasn't in love with her, why did *she* run away with *him*?"

"She was presumably under some compulsion, magical or

otherwise," I retorted. "I repeat—the question is, why did he take her with him, if he knew that his brother was in love with her?"

"He obviously needed her," Saint-Germain countered. "Or, to be strictly accurate, the egregore did. She was necessary to the magic he—or it—intended to work in Paris…magic that evidently took a great deal longer to prepare than he had antici- pated, in spite of his eventual recruitment of assistance from Puységur and the Harmonic Society. Presumably, he counted on drawing vital energy from others to preserve his life and strength…but something went badly awry. How did that happen, I wonder? Were they cursed by the witches they left behind in Campania? Did the effects of opposed evil eyes clash and sow destruction in all directions?"

"Those are certainly interesting questions," Dupin observed, scrupulously. "Unfortunately, those are matters on which Monsieur Fouché's multitudinous and conscientiously loqua- cious spies cast no light at all."

"But they testified that Paolo *was* in love with Maddalena?" I said, remembering his reaction when he awoke from the spell cast by the violin.

"They did. Which, as you were doubtless about to say, might help us to understand Paolo's motives in hastening to Paris as soon as news reached him of his brother's death. Fouché's spies reported that he had conceived an extremely strong sense of grievance against his brother, and that any further encounter between the two would undoubtedly have been fatal for one of them. Such is the efficiency of French state secrecy, however, that he had no idea where his brother was…until the dutiful French authorities—perhaps in the spirit of the left hand not quite knowing what the right was doing—notified him of his formal inheritance of the entailed family properties in Naples and Corsica. Obviously, he is intent on recovering both the cello and Maddalena…but exactly what his intentions are in either respect remains unclear, until we can ask him. He did, however, complete the necessary formalities in Marseille and at the Barrière. He was telling the truth when he told you that he did not kill Valdoni—the paperwork in question gives him an alibi."

"That *was* Maddalena, then?" Saint-Germain queried—although I didn't suppose that he doubted it any longer.

"Probably," was all that Dupin was prepared to say.

"Definitely," I said, dryly. "Maddalena tried to hire Valdoni, and subsequently killed him, in a fit of spite…acting of her own accord. She was able to get close enough to him to stab him because he had no fear of a seemingly-frail old woman. She knew, somehow, that he had come to warn you, and considered that a betrayal worthy of the ultimate revenge…unless, of course, she simply could not contain her anger."

Dupin frowned slightly, but did not attempt to question my certainty.

"But who or what has since taken control of the gypsy woman?" Saint-Germain demanded. "An egregore, presumably—but what kind? Is it merely a human being with magnetic powers, whether alive or recently returned from the dead? Or is it a disembodied creature, separate in itself from those it possesses?"

"The latter, surely," I said. "You can't really believe that Tommaso Angelotti has returned from the dead to enslave his housekeeper all over again. That's impossible, isn't it, Dupin?"

"At the stage, I still have an open mind," Dupin assured me.

"So have I, now," Saint-Germain retorted. "I have met real and powerful magic today—not for the first time in my life, by any means, but for the first time that left no possible room for doubt. I have always known that there was a true adept beneath my impostures, but I never knew for sure, until today, what a true adept might be capable of accomplishing. Destiny has brought me to this point, Dupin—and I know now what my presidency of the Harmonic Society is fated to achieve. I have been given a star to guide me."

"You might want to reflect on that a little more carefully before you come to any final decision about your own power, or the appropriate direction of your small army of petty mesmer-ists," Dupin opined.

"Don't quibble!" said Saint-Germain. "Do you or do you not believe that what we are confronted with here is an egregore?"

"Oh yes," said Dupin. "I'm sure of that, at least."

"And that the entity, whatever the detail of it might be, is powerful and dangerous?"

"Extremely so," Dupin agreed. "If the *entity*, as you put it, really were Michele Pezza reincarnate, then it might well hope to destroy Paris, and devastate France. Even if its intentions are less ambitious than that, they are probably destructive, and not on any trivial scale."

Saint-Germain blinked. "And you think it capable of wreaking such destruction as to destroy Paris?" he said, as if he could not quite believe that the man he considered to be a determined skeptic now seemed so credulous.

"I don't know," Dupin replied, "but I'd rather not find out the hard way, if that eventuality can possibly be nipped in the bud."

"When Paolo Mazzoli mentioned Pezza's name," I put in, "he also mentioned Cagliostro. I had made a careless reference to harmonies of hell, and he obviously recognized it as the title of a book—and knew that Cagliostro had paid for its printing."

"We already knew that Grigoryi and Balsamo were acquainted, back in the last century," Dupin said, dismissively, evidently of the opinion that it was a matter of little importance. "We need to concentrate on his more recent acquaintances—which brings us back to Dupotet. Are you sure, Saint-Germain, that he is the only other member of the Society with which Grigoryi was recently in contact?"

"Not absolutely certain," Saint-Germain admitted. "But he's by far the most likely candidate—except that, if Tommaso…I mean Grigoryi…had confided anything significant to him, he'd surely have given me some indication."

"Perhaps Dupotet is merely a dupe," I suggested.

"He's no fool, though," Dupin objected. "If he were made an accomplice to some insidious plan without being aware of it—

and without giving any indication of it to anyone else—it must have been cleverly done. Tell me, St Germain—does Dupotet own a piano?"

"Yes—a concert grand. He's no great player, though. He invites prestigious guests to play at his musical soirées…he's keenly ambitious to move up in society, as evidenced by the recent restyling of his name. But I don't understand why you're so obsessed with pianos—I have one myself, but Tommaso never showed any conspicuous interest in it."

"Do you invite prestigious guests to play at *your* soirées?" I murmured—but neither Saint-Germain nor Dupin took any notice.

"The reason I consider the piano to be potentially significant," Dupin explained, "is that I observed, in this very room, that Grigoryi Mazzoli, alias Thomas Angelotti, had taken the trouble to acquire sheet music for several sonatas scored for piano and cello—presumably by way of research, given that he could not possibly play either instrument. What we did not find, though, either here or at the house, was any music that Grigoryi might have composed, or attempted to compose. Nor did we find anything at all that he had written—although he *could* still write, in spite of his crippling arthritis, well enough to scribble the notes that Maddalena carried on his behalf.…"

"And you think that the Baron Du Potet's possession of a grand piano might have persuaded Tommaso to entrust his writings—his musical scores—to him rather than the Society… or me," Saint-Germain concluded for him, obligingly."

"I'm not sure that *entrusted* is the right word," Dupin said. "As I said, Dupotet is no fool, but every man has his weakness, which can render him exploitable. At any rate, our next step is obvious—we must go to see Duptotet."

"I'm not going haring off there right away," I put in, swiftly. "I need to get cleaned up first—and so do you, Saint-Germain. Unless we have some reason to think that Dupotet's in deadly danger, we can surely postpone our visit for an hour or two, at least?"

"I suppose we can," Dupin said. "In any case, I need to return home myself, to consult my books."

"*Les Harmonies de l'enfer*, no doubt?" Saint-Germain put in, not bothering to conceal the hint of resentment in his voice.

"Among others, yes," Dupin agreed.

"Does it have anything to say about severed hands?" Saint-Germain asked, sarcastically. "They couldn't do much with a cello or a fiddle, but I suppose one might play a piano, if it were active enough."

"I find that exceedingly hard to believe," Dupin opined, quite earnestly. "Without the muscles and tendons in the wrist, a severed hand would be impotent, no matter how active it might be. If I find any such reference, though, I'll be sure to let you know. My friend is right, I suppose: he does need to clean himself up…and so do you."

Saint-Germain did not dispute the fact; as soon as I had reminded him of the fact, he had begun to look down at himself, and touch the cloth of his various garments with reluctant fingers. The force of his recent revelation and the bizarrerie of the mystery enfolding us had obviously joined in competition with his dandy's sensibilities, and the latter seemed to be on the point of victory. He rang for Whalen, probably to instruct him to draw a hot bath. When the butler appeared, he was carrying the silver tray bearing the morning post, almost as if he thought that Saint-Germain's belated acceptance of it might constitute a sign of forgiveness for his earlier unwitting betrayal.

The soiled dandy was about to wave the tray away for a second time when something caught his eye, and he snatched up one of the letters from the spiral array, which had been carefully formulated so that any crests that appeared on the envelopes would be immediately visible.

Saint-Germain broke the seal on the letter and ripped it open so fiercely that the envelope tore in two—but the embossed card inside was made of sterner stuff.

"What is it?" Dupin asked, when Saint-Germain seemed momentarily incapable of speech.

Without saying a word, the President of the Harmonic Society handed over the invitation, which was addressed to him in exactly that capacity.

It was an invitation to attend a reception at the Baron Du Potet de Sennevoy's house, at eight o'clock that very evening, at which there would be a musical recital featuring a piano, a cello and female soprano, the program to include the première of a recently-composed nocturne. The name of the composer whose work was to be exposed for the first time was not recorded on the invitation, but the names of the performers were. The piano would be played by Frédéric Chopin and the cello by Félix Battanchon; the soprano would be Cornélie Falcon.

The appearance of two of those three names was verging on the sensational. Cornélie Falcon had not performed in public for more than three years, having supposedly ruined her allegedly-unique "dark soprano" voice by excessive effort in the course of a spectacular but tragically brief career. Chopin was supposed to be very ill, and it had not been expected that he would play in public again—certainly not to play the work of another composer. Most recipients of the invitation would, therefore have taken the inference that the nocturne whose première was being advertised was his—although Saint-Germain had already jumped to a different conclusion, as I had myself.

Even Dupin recognised Chopin's name, and that of Mademoiselle Falcon, but he had to ask who Battachon was—and he addressed the question to Saint-Germain, evidently suspecting some Mesmeric connection.

"He's the leading cellist at the Grand Opéra," Saint-Germain told him. "Quite possibly the finest in Paris—and hence the finest in the world."

"Ah," was Dupin's reflective reply. He did not need to add the explanatory remark that all music—including, and especially, music intended to have a profound effect on the human mind—is more effective by far when played by performers of genius.

The Comte turned to Whalen again, and the butler shrank before his master's unexpectedly-renewed wrath. "When did this letter arrive?" he demanded.

"This morning, sir!" Whalen replied, mortally insulted by the tacit suggestion that he might have been dilatory in completing its delivery.

Saint-Germain took his word for it. "The swine!" he muttered. "He must have sent it out late deliberately, so as not to give me forewarning—perhaps in the hope that the notice would be too short to allow me to attend. Mazzoli *has* subverted him, more thoroughly than I would have thought possible... and the egregore's scheme is much further advanced than we thought. No wonder Maddalena was in such a hurry to recover the magical cello...Du Potet was probably intended to collect it from the house himself."

I look at Dupin and raised an eyebrow by way of commentary. Saint-Germain's larcenous instincts had obviously caused his grasp to exceed his reach. Dupin looked back, rather blankly.

"If I had posed as a Baron instead of a Comte," Saint-Germain continued, still muttering, "perhaps I could have assembled a trio like that for one of my recitals...with a little assistance from a vampiric monster avid for a soul-sucking feast."

"Do you suppose I've got one of those invitations waiting for me in the vestibule at home?" I asked, in a tone that had more amusement in it than anxiety, although I was not sure why.

"It doesn't matter," Saint-Germain said, dully. "I don't suppose Du Potet will be able to object if I bring you two along as my guests—after all, he has a very large garden, and you have been previously introduced to him."

CHAPTER TEN
REFRESHING THE BODY
AND THE MIND

Although I had no butler to draw my bath it did not take long to clean myself up, put on fresh clothes and eat a hearty, if rather belated, breakfast in order to soothe my raging appetite. Fortunately, although there was no invitation to the Baron Du Potet de Sennevoy's soirée waiting in my vestibule, the delivery from the local bakery had been made, and my larder was very well-stocked with preserves. Given the exertions of the previous night, I ought to have felt tired thereafter, but in fact I was wide awake and full of energy, although the black coffee with which I dosed myself copiously presumably assisted that sensation. Indeed, I felt better than I had for weeks; the oppression of the summer heat actually seemed to have lifted somewhat

Perhaps, I thought, *I'm finally adapting myself to the fifth element that haunts this time of year.*

When my body was fully refreshed, I immediately began searching the recesses of my desk for the manuscript I had written three years before, and to which I had hardly given a thought since: the account of Dupin's encounter with the "spoiled Stradivarius."

To some extent, the story I had written down only confirmed what I had already remembered about the murders committed during performances of a play called *The Devil's Sonata*, written by Frédéric Soulié, with music by Maurice Bazailles. The play had been based on Guiseppe Tartini's account of composing *Il*

Trillo de Diavolo after a dream in which the Devil had played a much finer tune to him, and the theater orchestra had featured a Stradivarius once allegedly owned by Tartini, having been gifted to him by the famous luthier, who thought it unfit for sale. It had seemed to me to be perfectly evident, at the time, that the boy soprano who had sung the crucial solo had been under some malevolent supernatural—yes, *supernatural*—influence focused in the violin, which had also tried to possess Dupin when he had been compelled to play it, while the boy sang to its accompaniment. What might have happened had Dupin not defeated the influence in question, I had no idea—but even Dupin had been prepared to admit, frankly, that it had threatened to open a gap between the world that we know as a reality and another: a "dream-dimension" subject to the dominion, or at least the influence, of an "unwholesome" force or entity that *Les Harmonies de l'enfer* called Nyarlathotep, the Crawling Chaos.

The more interesting reward of my re-reading, however, lay in certain incidental details of the commentary, especially with respect to the effects of music on the human mind—specifically, the suggestion that music's ability to reflect and induce powerful emotions results from its appeal to aspects of mind more fundamental than consciousness, and perhaps more fundamental than the materiality of the flesh, and the corollary assertion that music might be capable of providing a spiritual path to an ecstatic and paradisal state of mind...or its infernal counterpart.

"Fascinating," I murmured, almost as if I were reading the piece for the first time, and experiencing something akin to a revelation.

I had also recorded a judgment that Dupin had repeated to me several times since, in other contexts—that consciousness is not a mere collector of sensory experience but an active composer a seeker and synthesizer of harmonies, always in quest of something that remains tantalizingly out of reach—and the further suggestion that consciousness might be reckoned as a kind of refuge from the dangerous tendencies of the imagination: that "in our waking lives we are fugitives." That was an opinion I had reiterated myself, only a few days earlier, in making the observation that Dupin seemed, in his waking life, without quite being aware of it, to be avoiding music in general, and certain kinds of music in particular. I wondered whether he, too, might have forgotten the episode in the house in the Rue d'Auseuil, or at least put it out of his mind—until now.

Now that he had been obliged by circumstance to consult *Les Harmonies de l'enfer* again, I wondered, and forced to focus once again on the knotty problem of how much truth it contained, how much deception and how much misconception, how well would he be armed and armored for a contest? Was he still as powerful as he had been in the Rue d'Auseuil? If so, would his adversary, this time, prove as vulnerable to his counter-assault?

That was by no means the only thing I wondered, of course.

How narrow an escape had I had that afternoon when Maddalena had failed to harmonize her voice with the glissando she had played on the guitar? How close had the boundaries of reality been to breaking down outside as well as within my fugitive consciousness? How well would I be armed and armoured myself for the inevitable contest to come?

Presumably, I thought, I would have had to be reckoned collateral damage if the psychic blast of Maddalena's violin had killed me, because its primary target must have been Paolo Mazzoli—but I would not have been any less dead. That whole episode, however, had been a late addendum to whatever plan was being hatched here—a mere sideswipe, intended to get rid of a minor annoyance. The principal reality-breaching performance was surely scheduled for tonight, when something infinitely more profound would be involved than mere "gypsy fiddling".

Would Cornélie Falcon's supposedly-ruined voice be able to carry the performance any better than Maddalena's, though? Might it not have been safer to select a lesser but more reliable performer—Mademoiselle Deurne, for example? And what if

Chopin's illness got the better of him, making it impossible for him to complete his performance? Of the three, it seemed to me that only Battanchon was a safe bet. What was Dupotet thinking?

Except, of course, that he was probably not the one doing the thinking; this performance had to have been planned by Grigoryi Mazzoli...or by the egregore that had been in possession of his frail and impotent body for such a long time, and incarnate in the cello too.

I had no doubt that *egregoroi* were, by nature, patient entities—but how frustrating it must have been to be so patient with weakness for so long, and then to lose its principal instrument to the everyday ravages of human mortality, with the prospect of renewed power once again in sight! Perhaps, if it had not been for the deadly heat of high summer, Grigoryi might have lasted another month or so...long enough, at any rate, to see the scheme through to completion. He had survived July, but August had obvously been too much for him....

I could not imagine that the Baron Du Potet de Sennevoy was an informed accomplice of whatever scheme the egregore was about to bring to fruition, but I guessed that he had been willing enough, and that the mere fact of being able to assemble the remarkable trio must have boosted his avid self-esteem enormously. I had enough experience of Mesmerists by now to know that the more ambitious they were, the more vulnerable they were to being gulled. If common-or-garden confidence tricksters like the Comte de Saint-Germain and Jana Valdemar had already fooled Dupotet, as they obviously had, what chance would he stand against authentic magical power? And if Saint-Germain and Mademoiselle Valdemar were so ready to fall for their own line of patter, how much more vulnerable must the ambitious Baron have been?

It had to take place in August, I thought, *else performers of that caliber would not have been free to attend a mere soirée in the faubourgs. And it had to be this August, or Chopin and Cornélie Facon would have left the city with everyone else, instead of being delayed here by illness or the determination to prepare for a return to the stage...not to mention the fact that, as recently as last year, the Mesmerist who now styles himself the Baron Du Potet de Sennevoy was merely Monsieur Dupotet, a humble researcher at the Saltpêtrière. Tonight, the stars are right, in more ways than one.*

My eyes were drawn back to the manuscript then: to something else I had recorded, almost casually, when attempting to describe what had happened in that attic in the Rue d'Auseuil: that the "singing of the chaos-spawn" was slow and deep—far lower in pitch, I now supposed, than any note played on a violin could hope to reach...something more akin, perhaps, to the register of a bass cello.

But exactly what kind of entity—what kind of *egregore*—was it that now had Maddalena in its merciless grasp, as Grigoryi Mazzoli must once have had her in his thrall, in order to steal away from her supposedly true lover? And exactly what did it plan to accomplish, now that it apparently had the particular instruments it wanted, the particular players it wanted—and, presumably, the particular music it required?

I didn't know—and I felt strangely frustrated by my ignorance...as if the answer were within my reach if I only knew how to release the secret catch that held it prisoner.

I might have continued that reverie for some considerable time, without achieving any more than vague frustration, oddly coupled with mild amusement, but the doorbell rang. I went to answer it, putting the manuscript back in the drawer where I had hidden it.

I was not surprised to find that the caller was Dupin. It was more than two hours before the time at which Saint-Germain had promised to pick us up in his carriage, in order that we might hold a brief council of war before we all went together to Dupotet's house, but there was every reason why Dupin would want to confer with me in advance, by way of forewarning. He had not trusted Saint-Germain before, and now that Saint-Germain claimed to have had a revelation to the effect that he really was the person he was pretending to be—a person who might never have existed at all—there seemed to be even less reason to anticipate that he could or would be of any help in saving Paris from disaster, if Paris did stand in need of salvation.

I sat Dupin down in his customary chair in the smoking room, and offered him a bandy and a cigar. He accepted the cigar but refused the brandy. "I need my mind to be sharp," he told me. "I might risk a glass of champagne at Dupotet's reception, in the interests of blending in, but nothing stronger."

I looked him up and down, but did not offer the comment that his chances of "blending in" at a quasi-aristocratic salon, where aspirant dandies would be out in force, were a trifle remote. Even mine did not seem strong, although I suspected that I had spent more on my waistcoat than he had on his entire outfit, hat and gloves included.

"Have you found out anything more?" I asked him.

"*Found* out would be a trifle excessive," he said, puling his pedantic face. "Even *figured* out might be over-exaggerated— but I have certainly assembled a chain of conjectures that might be of some assistance to us. You were right, by the way."

"About what?"

"About the lack of wisdom in my neglect of contemporary music. That was foolish. I had forgotten, or set aside, one of my own principles—that history is progress. Music makes progress, just as science does, in all aspects of its technics: its instruments, its notation, its theory and its artistry. The lyre of Orpheus was a effective instrument in many ways—for which we might have cause to be grateful, if his reputation as a player and singer was not exaggerated—but we have progressed far beyond *citheras* now. Our singers are better-trained, and our composers more ingenious by far…but I had never paused to consider that we might be approaching a climacteric of sorts, which was bound to bring opportunists crawling out of the woodwork in unprecedented numbers."

"The affair of the spoiled Stradivarius should have reminded you if the everpresence of the *Harmonies de l'enfer* on your bookshelves did not," I said, daring for once to be critical.

"You're right," he said, again. "At the time, that seemed to me be something reaching out from the past—*my* past—and once it had been put away, I made the mistake of relegating it to the past, as if it were something I had settled and concluded...but the past is the springboard of the future, and one should always look forward as well as back."

"Is it chaos-spawn with which we have to deal again?" he asked.

"I doubt it," he answered, with a sight sigh—as if that might have been the preferable option. "Nor is it the dwellers on the thresholds, which can be contained if one can face up to them bravely. No, this is something that has been on Earth far longer than any momentary and blindly destructive invader; wherever it originated, it has adapted over time to our reality, and may be more purposive in consequence."

"An egregore?"

"Indeed. Unfortunately, such textual sources as there are cannot agree as to exactly what *egregoroi* are. The Biblical and Apocryphal references are misleading, of course, as are all such references to entities that the guardians of the new faiths were trying to expunge from consciousness, or redefine as demons. Even so, the references are not uninteresting; the parents of the nephilim were initially defined as angels rather than demons, even though the conclusion was eventually drawn that they must have been fallen angels, condemned to Pandemonium for their fornication with the daughters of men. More recent references, however, suggest that fornication is only peripherally involved, if at all."

"Saint-Germain says that an egregore is a kind of psychic vampire," I told him, obligingly. "Either a human individual who sets out to drain another by means of a psychic link, or an independent entity formed as a result of some such fusion of minds, which then begins to drain all its creators."

"So the modern texts assert—but the interesting thing about

the assertion is the manner in which the linkage is supposedly formed."

"By music?"

"By music, indeed—but not in any simple sense. Even in the straightforward instances where one individual is alleged to benefit at another's expense, drawing strength, health and perhaps youth from the other, the process is peculiar. For one thing, the egregore does not play—it is a surrogate or a victim who plays the instrument, having been seduced into that determination by the would-be vampire; for another, there are always more than two individuals involved. In conventional vampire mythology, predation is usually sexual, literally or metaphorically: female vampires are supposed to prey routinely upon males, and vice versa, usually employing extraordinary sexual attraction as a lure. Although there are not many recorded instances of supposed egregoric predation, those that are recorded involve males preying upon other males—usually with a female accomplice, who accompanies the victim and a second instrumentalist as a singer. The female accomplice is not represented as a seductress or the victim of erotic seduction, but merely as a pawn, held in thrall by one or both of the males—although she too is said to benefit from the exchange of energy. In those instances where the egregore is represented as an independent entity, its male instrument is in thrall too, being employed as a conduit through which psychic energy is chaneled to the ultimate recipient, benefiting himself only as a side-effect, in much the same way that the female accomplice benefits."

"Very complicated," I observed, "and very odd."

"Even odder, I fear, when we try to fit the present individuals into the pattern. We may presume, I suppose, that Grigoryi Mazzoli conceived vampiric ambitions of his own after playing his part on Michele Pezza's diplomatic and symbolic pact with the Devil—aiming, as most ambitious individuals of that sort do, for a means to prolong his life and acquire an easy prosperity. Obviously, he had some additional source of inspiration, which apparently gave him something in common with Giuseppe Balsamo, alias Cagliostro. Given that it was Cagliostro who caused a few copies of *Les Harmonies de l'enfer* to be printed in Paris some sixty years ago, I'm inclined to guess that Mazzoli had read the manuscript too. In all probability, both were members of some secret society of Masonic magicians—such societies were rife at the end of the last century, as the decadence of the *ancien régime* reached its apogee in France and the last remnants of Renaissance glory were evaporating in the Italian city states.

"Grigoryi Mazzoli would not have been alone in deciding that the residue of pagan witchcraft contained in the folklore of stubbornly-uncivilized Europe might be fruitfully combined with the scholarly magic of civilized Europe in such a way as to acquire, or reacquire, a useful hybrid vigor. Perhaps he had some kind of revelation during the rite at which the supposed diabolical pact was sealed, akin to the one that Saint-Germain believes he experienced today. At any rate, he must have become convinced that he had an instrument in his custody—the Guadagnini cello—that could out-perform the hill-folk's violins in their various supposedly magical operations, and he set out to supplement its potential power with the appropriate accessories."

"Maddalena."

"Yes. I presume that she was an accomplished violin-player even then...and, more crucially, a fine singer."

"And a beauty, if a well-born youth like Paolo Mazzoli became besotted with her," I said thoughtfully. "So what happened to her to turn her into an apparent deaf-mute and an old crone?"

"Probably the same thing that happened to Grigoryi's fingers."

"Arthritis?" I said, momentarily bewildered.

"*Malocchio*—the evil eye. Or, I suspect, *jettatura*."

"I thought they were the same thing—and I didn't know that you believed in such things."

"I'm not convinced that curses have any objective power of

their own to hurt people—but I'm quite certain that people who believe that they have been cursed may suffer the symptoms of the curse, especially if they believe the curse to have been deserved."

"Falling for their own line of patter, assisted by a guilty conscience?"

"It cuts deeper than that. As I've said before, the human mind is a composer, not a collector; it creates the fabric of belief rather than merely inducing it from genuine patterns in sensory experience. Consciousness is so configured that it is very hard to *disbelieve* in curses—as I think you know well enough, following your experience with *The Mad Trist*."

In fact, I thought I was doing rather well in coping with the problem of disbelief, in that particular matter—but it was not one I cared to talk about. "What's the difference, then?" I asked. "Between *malocchio* and *jettatura*, that is."

"To simplify it brutally, *malocchio* is controllable; *jettatura* is not. A witch who has the power of *malocchio* may use it as he or she wishes, but to be a *jettatura* is a curse in itself, because a *jettatura* cannot help afflicting those close to him or her with a progressive decline into decrepitude, which may be painfully long-drawn-out."

"So you think Grigoryi Mazzoli was a *jettatura*—or, at least, that Maddalena came to believe that he was?"

"Yes—and I suspect that she was a *jettatura* too…or, at least, that he came to believe that she was. Theirs was a *folie à deux*."

"My God! Why on earth, in that case, would they stay together?"

"Perhaps because they needed one another, regardless of the cost…or believed that they did…and perhaps because they thought that they might be able to reverse the damage done, if they could only find a way to manifest the power that Grigoryi believed he had: by discovering and controlling a player, or group of players, who might serve as an instrument of their predation."

"You'd think they might have given up after forty years

without success," I observed.

"We don't know for sure that they had no success," Dupin said, mildly. "We don't know how many other young men Grigoryi Mazzoli might have befriended, before Dupotet and Saint-Germain. They didn't contrive to reverse their decrepitude, but they did keep themselves alive."

"And the egregore too," I suggested. "Assuming that it is the kind of egregore that exists independently of its human possessions, sustained by the psychic energy leeched by its human instruments, leaving them just enough to maintain their usefulness as instruments...prolonging their lives, but not necessarily their joys."

"But Grigoryi Mazzoli is dead now," Dupin observed. "He lived for a long time, albeit by no means prosperously, but death claimed him in the end...and his precious cello was snatched from his home, on behalf of the Harmonic Philosophical Society of Paris...."

"Temporarily," I countered. "And he lived long enough to see the egregore's plan through to the very brink of completion. Although it's also possible, I suppose, that what Saint-Germain and I saw in the catacombs this morning gave rise to a misleading impression. Appearances suggested that Maddalena was a mere puppet, just as the Neapolitan brigands her music possessed became puppets—but that might have been mere appearance. She, and she alone, might be the egregore, even if she has come to believe that there's some other, disembodied entity pulling her strings...."

"That's possible," Dupin conceded, warily.

"Whether that's the case or not," I added, "the music she played in the catacombs had real power, and it nearly killed us all in spite of its imperfections. If the music that is scheduled to be played at Dupotet's salon tonight came from the same source, and the instruments are capable of supporting it...it will surely be all the more powerful in consequence."

"It surely will," Dupin agreed. "To the extent that music can be magic...and we would be foolish to underestimate that extent, given what we know from experience…the one thing of which we *can* be sure is that modern instruments, played by properly-trained performers, are capable of making more powerful magic than lyres, tambours and untrained singers. If nothing else, the cello is capable of playing a true *portamento*, which no lyre ever was. Even Giuseppe Tartini, convinced that he was doing all he could to duplicate the Devil's music, only employed trills."

"Does the significance of *glissando* and *portamento* lie entirely in their disruptive potential?" I asked. "I believe that similar moves have been used in German baroque music to symbolize Christ's descent to earth and ascent to heaven— neither of which is a step toward chaos or oblivion. Is it possible that *glissando* might be employed as a means to paradisal ecstasy instead of infernal corruption?"

"That's possible too," Dupin admitted.

"Is it possible, then," I wondered aloud, "that we are mistaking the ultimate goal of the egregore that had Grigoryi Mazzoli in its possession, and *egregoroi* in general? Saint-Germain insists on talking in terms of vampirism, parasitism and predation, and Maddalena, like Michele Pezza before her, may be constrained to think in terms of witchcraft and diabolism for want of any better—but even she and he wanted the Devil to serve a cause they considered just and benign. Perhaps the egregore's ultimate aims are virtuous."

"There is no doubt that it is murderous," Dupin pointed out. "Maddalena is a killer, and Pezza—no matter how just he considered his cause to be—was certainly a very violent man, capable of extraordinary cruelty."

"If an egregore's intellect and emotions originate in its human possessions," I argued, "then it is perfectly understandable that it is capable of vengeful spite and violence concomitant to ambition…but there has been progress in human history and human intelligence, has there not? Why should there not be progress in an egregore's development too? Is it not one of your tenets that there is progress in all things? For whatever reason, *this* egregore has been in Paris for forty years, many of them spent in the bosom of the Harmonic Philosophical Society…which is not the Académie, to be sure, but is not so very different in its outlook and ambition….."

"You might be right," Dupin conceded, grudgingly. "But we can hardly take its progress or good intentions on trust, can we? We have seen no sign of charity at all, but only of murder—and needless murder at that. What you say about the use of pitch-changes in German baroque music may be true, and the Infinities to which such effects point may not always be distressing. Let us not forget, though, that for every Christ, there is a vast host of anti-Christs. Goodness is rare; evil, alas, is commonplace… and *glissando* is intrinsically disturbing. Whether music has meaning in and of itself is, I suppose, a matter for metaphysical debate, but when the human ear hears it, consciousness certainly makes meaning out of it, and the meaning that consciousness cannot help but attribute to *glissando*, as the cognitive embedding of what the ears record is progressively negated by the slide in pitch, is an ominous one. Whether such musical devices can shatter the bounds of reality in any objective sense, I beg leave to doubt—but I also beg leave to doubt whether there is any objective sense in which we can speak about reality. If matter is the possibility of perception, as the idealists assert, then *glissando*, by affecting our consciousness of the harmony of existence, can threaten existence itself. In the right circumstances, it can kill—and might do worse. The possibility that it might do good instead, even if it were deployed with good intentions, is—in my opinion—remote."

"But you don't really think that the egregore, even if it were moved by the undead spirit of Michele Pezza, intends to use Dupotet's recital to send some kind of lethal blast across the whole of Paris?"

"Not in any crude sense, no. I'm not convinced that Pezza's role in this was ever more than peripheral—but you can probably imagine better than I can the kind of audience that Dupotet's promised treat will attract, even though the greater part of the

Parisian *haut monde* has deserted the city for the coast or the mountains. Exactly what effect the music is intended to have on them, I cannot say as yet, but if it involves the leaching of their psychic energy—their strength, their courage, their intelligence and their talent—it might leave a scar that is no less deep for being hardly visible. Louis-Philippe will not attend in person, but if his administration is as rickety as rumor suggests, and Revolution really is in the air…well, even if the egregore's intentions are merely gluttonous, and have no political component whatsoever, its success might well have political ramifications."

"Is there anything we can do to stop it, though?" I asked. "I can't see any way that we can prevent Grigoryi Mazzoli's composition from being played tonight—after all, we can't simply ask Dupotet to call it off, can we? And if we try to interfere with the performance in any way, Dupotet's guests will think we're insane and act accordingly"

"True," Dupin conceded. "But the egregore's scheme is not yet complete, and you've already remarked on its excessive and seemingly-perverse complication. Had the matter been simple, Grigoryi Mazzoli might have arranged matters to his satisfaction forty years ago; the mere fact that his adventure has dragged on for so long offers us hope that it might be frustrated yet again… perhaps indefinitely. And whatever happens, we surely ought not to miss out on tonight's performance, which promises to be a once-in-a-lifetime opportunity. If, as you have suggested, I have been direly neglectful in paying too little attention to contemporary music, I can think of no better opportunity to begin repairing the omission."

I was slightly startled by that, and raised the obvious objection. "But what if *you* were to fall victim to the egregore?" I asked. "What if *you* were to be sucked dry of your vital energy: not merely your strength, but your courage, your intelligence and your talent?"

"It might well be a stern test of my resistance," he said equably, "But it is, after all, but one more contest of reason and superstition…and if reason deserves its victory, then reason will surely win."

"Even when pitched against an authentically supernatural power?" I objected.

"As you know very well," he said, "I regard the term *super-natural* to be devoid of meaning. However strange and perverse *egregoroi* might be, given that such things really exist, they must be reckoned natural, and if they are natural, then reason may contend with them…and win."

I looked him directly in the eyes then, and said: "I can't believe that."

He met my stare frankly, and replied: "It would be better, my friend, if you could—for you will be exposed to danger too, if this performance does take place as planned, and the music that is played really can reach into the inner depths of our being."

CHAPTER ELEVEN
PAOLO MAZZOLI'S LUST
FOR VENGEANCE

Saint-Germain's coachman came to the door at the agreed time to tell us that his master was waiting in his carriage. We had left a considerable interval in hand, in order that we might at least discuss the situation, if not come up with some tentative agreement as to how we might proceed once we reached the Baron's house, although we had not specified exactly where that discussion would take place. I had thought that Saint-Germain might come into the house, and that we might simply continue the discussion that Dupin and I had already begun in the smoking-room, but there seemed to be no particular reason why we should not sit in the carriage instead, or allow the Mesmerist's coachman to drive us to some suitably comfortable restaurant or tavern—until I actually opened the carriage door in order to step up into the vehicle, and saw that Saint-Germain was not alone.

For a moment, I thought his companion might be Donatien, who had finally found his way home again after being abandoned unconscious in the alleyway near Les Halles, but it was not.

It was Paolo Mazzoli—and Mazzoli was holding a gun.

The gun was not an American revolver, and only seemed to be capable of firing two shots before being reloaded, but it was a fearsome weapon nevertheless.

"Don't worry, my friends," Saint-Germain was quick to

say. "Signor Mazzoli does not intend to kill any of us—he is merely holding the gun in his hand by way of demonstration, and to make himself feel a little more secure. This afternoon's experience has left a rather deep impression on him, and he is nursing an irrepressible terror as well as a fierce resentment. His remaining associates have fled—quite understandably—and he is all alone…except for us."

I climbed into the carriage, after the merest hesitation, and then offered my hand to Dupin to help him climb up too. We took our seats opposite Saint-Germain and Mazzoli, with our backs to the coachman. Saint-Germain's carriage was roomy and well-upholstered, as befitted a man of his social pretensions; it was also quite well-lit, by a miniature bull's-eye lantern suspended from the center of the ceiling.

"Dupotet will surely consider that you're overstepping the bounds of permissible unconventionality if you introduce *three* additional guests to his soirée," I observed, censoriously. "One would be easily acceptable, two stretching a point, but three…."

"Given his blatant rudeness in not sending my invitation in good time," Saint-Germain observed, "I am not conscience-stricken. He ought to be—but he cannot refuse us admission, in any case, without making a scene."

"What kind of gun is that?" Dupin asked, with typical mildness. "I've never seen one like it before."

"This," said Paolo Mazzoli proudly, as Saint-Germain rapped on the wall next to my head the knob of his cane, and the carriage drew away, "is what the English in India call a howdah gun. Effectively, it's a pistol-sized version of a double-barreled shotgun, which fires large-calibre cartridges through a short, unrifled barrel. Accurate aiming is impossible, but it's intended for use at point-blank range…and it's intended to blast its target into bloody shreds. The English, as you probably know, like to hunt tiger from the relative safety of an elephant's back—but they also like to keep a weapon of last resort, in case a tiger contrives to reach them even there. This is supposed to be fired into the leaping tiger's gaping maw."

"It must make a terrible mess of the animal's pelt," I observed.

"Imagine what it must do to the animal's brain," was the Neapolitan's retort.

"And at whom do you intend to discharge it?" Dupin inquired.

"Not at whom—at what."

"Ah!" I said. "Have you given up on your quest to obtain possession of the Guadagnini cello, then? You've decided to destroy it instead, in a fit of pique."

"Why do you think I wanted it in the first place?" Mazzoli countered.

Saint-Germain undertook to answer that on his behalf. "We were wrong, apparently, to assume that Paolo had the same ambitions as his brother...and what I've told him about the life that his brother and Maddalena actually lived in Paris, coupled with what he observed in the catacombs, has only served to increase his hatred of the instrument, to which he attributes three heinous crimes."

"Three?" I queried.

"The betrayal of Michele Pezza, and the betrayal of the hopes that his brother and Maddalena entertained, in consequence of that treason," Saint-Germain explained. Obviously, he considered Maddalena's three murders to be trivial matters. "He believes the instrument to be haunted by an evil spirit...an egregore."

"Shut up!" said Mazzoli, sharply. "You don't know what you're talking about. You don't have the slightest idea what we're dealing with here."

"Nor do you, if you think you can simply blast it apart with a *howdah gun*," Saint-Germain riposted. Evidently, whatever uneasily alliance the two had formed was by no means entirely harmonious. "If you really expect me to gain admittance to the Baron's recital for you, you really must leave that thing in the carriage. Even if you can conceal it about your person, which I doubt, and even if you could somehow contrive to aim it at the instrument without endangering its player, you'd be wrestled to the ground the moment you took it out. The Prefect of Police is going to be present, for God's sake, and half a dozen députés. Every liveried servant there will be a policeman in disguise, and there'll be a dozen more lurking in the garden. You're a Neapolitan—do you have any idea how many eyes will be glued to you the moment you step through the door? The fact that you've been introduced by the President of the Philosophical Harmonic Society of Paris won't help, believe me. The Baron might owe me some deference and consideration, now that he's a loyal member of the Inner Circle, but Monsieur Groix has a very different opinion of me—thanks to *you*, Dupin."

"Monsieur Groix is perfectly capable of making up his own mind about citizens in whom he takes an interest," Dupin observed, quietly, "and as it happens, your name has never come up in the course of our conversations. Thank you for introducing me, though—Auguste Dupin at your service, Monsieur Mazzoli."

"At my service?" Mazzoli repeated, as if he doubted that very much—as I did.

"Unfortunately," Dupin went on, speaking to the Neapolitan, "I have to agree with Monsieur le Comte. Your tiger-gun is unlikely to be deployable in this particular contest. If you really do want to prevent the cello from doing its work, you might do better to help us formulate a subtler plan."

"You don't know what you're talking about, any more than *he* does," the silver-haired man replied, intemperately.

"I have the only copy of *Les Harmonies de l'enfer* in Paris," Dupin informed him, "and I have been re-reading it within the last few hours. It's strange how easy it is to forget what one has read; it almost seemed to me that I was reading some of its passages for the first time, even though I was convinced that I had taken all the education from the text that I could. It's direly unreliable, of course, but with respect to that particular source, I can confidently say that I know as much as you do. As for Parthenope and the Opici…well, I have other sources. You might well believe that you know more about that than I do, having been party to Pezza's pact, but…well, I can assure you that I *do* know what I am talking about, insofar as anyone can know anything about such matters."

The light of the bull's-eye displayed Paolo Mazzoli's wide-eyed stare in all its haggard glory. I could see the terror that Saint-Germain had mentioned, as well as the astonishment that Dupin had just occasioned. As a Neapolitan, Mazzoli had never heard Dupin's name before, and knew nothing of his reputation, which was still esoteric even in Paris, in spite of the publicity given to it by my American friend. I took considerable satisfaction from the reflected glory in which I was able to bathe, although I could not help feeling slightly resentful that Dupin had obviously not had time to tell me everything that he had learned before we boarded the carriage.

"You know what kind of Devil it was with whom Michele made his pact?" Mazzoli said, incredulously.

"I would not use the word *know*, based on such dubious evidence," Dupin told him, "But I have formed a hypothesis as to the nature of the *egregoroi*, and their relationship with the sirens."

"Sirens?" Saint-Germain interjected. "What sirens?"

"The sirens of Greek myth," Dupin said, mildly, "which lured men to their doom with their voices, but were thwarted by Orpheus when they threatened to waylay the *Argo*. In particular, the siren Parthenope, who was said to have drowned herself for love of Odysseus—another potential victim who had guile enough to counter her charm."

"Greek myth?" Saint-Germain repeated, incredulously, although he was too vain a mock-intellectual to admit that he was out of his depth, and was quick to add: "A fine repository of wisdom, for those who know how to read it."

"Go on," said Mazzoli, warily.

"The name of the city of Naples is derived from the Greek Neapolis, which means *new town*," Dupin continued. "The original Neapolis was built alongside an earlier Greek colony on the Italian shore, named Parthenope—the name subsequently attributed to the siren, who was thought to have dwelt nearby.

In time, the new town absorbed the old, as new things are ever apt to do…although the old tend to persist, however fugitively. The people who lived in the region that the Romans eventually called Campania before the Greek colonists arrived were the Opici. The tribe was given several other names by the Greeks and Romans alike, who were never clear as to their exact identity, or the extent of their distinction from the Samnites, a rival tribe that provided much sterner opposition to all invaders of southern Italy. Like the city of Parthenope, the Opici were absorbed and seemingly obliterated…but the old tends to persist, alongside or within the body of the new….and that persistence can be stubborn.

"In theory, the Opici no longer existed by the time the Macedonian Empire extended its reach to embrace Neapolis and Parthenope, to be followed by the Roman Empire, and the Ostrogothic Kingdom, and the Byzantine Exarchate of Ravenna, and the Norman Kingdom of Sicily, and the Swabian Overlords, and the Papacy…and all the other multitudinous rulers who held temporary sway over Campania before the Bourbons came to seize it from the Spanish. It was then that Michele Pezza became the embodiment of a strange kind of patriotism: a kind that tried to shore itself up by reconnecting with the ultimate roots of Campanian culture…the myth and magic of the Opici, which had opposed itself nearly three thousand years before to the first so-called Parthenopean Republic. It was a very modern thing to do, of course, fully in tune with the ideas and ideals of the Romantic Movements that were sweeping Europe at the time, appealing as much to the educated elites of the Italian States as to those of Germany, France and England. That is how your brother became involved, I imagine—as a protégé of Giuseppe Balsamo, and a reader of *Les Harmonies de l'enfer*…which must have seemed just as Romantic, in its way, as Michele Pezza's silly patriotism."

"Silly?" Mazzoli objected, evidently feeling that there had been nothing silly about it.

"Yes, silly," said Dupin. "What was there, after all, to which a man like him—or you—could really be loyal? The French Naples, the Spanish Naples, the German Naples, the Norman Naples, the Roman Naples or the Greek Naples?…all of them, in their various ways, new, and all of them, in their various ways, false? Did you really think that making a treaty with the last fugitive remnants of the Opici would be any more authentic? Did your brother ever really think that mastery of the magic of the sirens, even if he could achieve it, would merely serve to grant him long life and the power to drain other men of their life-force to his own advantage? Yes, Signor Mazzoli—*silly*. As silly as your attempted blackmail in the catacombs. As silly as your ridiculous tiger-gun. As silly, I presume, as the egregore itself, which also has no conception of the hard reality of the world, or what the consequences might be of inducing a crack in that reality."

Mazzoli seemed to be speechless, and certainly did not seem inclined to charge Dupin once again with not knowing what he was talking about. Even Saint-Germain seemed confounded by the sheer mass of information and allegation—but I was deeply intrigued, and eager to know more.

"You think the egregore is *silly?*" I queried. "But its power… its magic…is very real, is it not?"

"Oh yes," he replied. "Its power is very real, whether we attribute it to magic or not. Its musical sensibility is real, and any music that it has composed will be all the more forceful for being scored for modern instruments and performed by contemporary instruments. Insofar as music has the power to affect the human mind, the concert that Dupotet has scheduled for tonight, presumably at the egregore's instigation, will be far more effective than Parthenope and her sister sirens ever were, and I doubt that Orpheus or Oyssesus would be capable of withstanding its force…but none of that is inconsistent with the hypothesis that the egregore is, in intellectual terms, a moron…a cretin…an idiot."

I wanted to strangle him, but gave no evidence of the fact. To distract myself, I looked out of the carriage window. We had just passed the Luxembourg gardens and were heading in the direction of the Observatoire. Perhaps it was the effect of the hill, or merely that of the wind created by the carriage's movement, but the sullen atmosphere seemed a little fresher, almost teasing in the way it tickled my beard and eyebrows. I was sitting on the right-hand side of the coach, facing the sunset, but there was not enough cloud in the sky to contrive a bloody display; the sun, not yet delicately balanced on the horizon, was still bright orange, and the sky around it a dazzling blue, with the merest hint of purple.

My ears were avid, though, and never missed a word.

"What else could be expected of something as ancient as the *egregoroi*," Dupin continued, "which have spent thousands of years parasitizing human ignorance and superstition, reliant on the crudest and most primitive consciousness and belief? They might have musical genius, as untutored tribesmen may have musical genius, but they cannot be party to the full rewards of philosophy and education. Do you really think, given such burden of inheritance, that a mere forty years leeching on the likes of Michele Pezza, Grigoryi Mazzoli and Maddalena can have taught the particular egregore with which we are dealing to understand and contend with modern existence? Indeed, rather than benefit from whatever meager wisdom those individuals might have had to begin with, it seems to have contrived to render them almost as stupid as itself. It took *forty years* for Grigoryi to complete his composition, even with the benefit of the egregore's inspiration, and to persuade Dupotet to have it played...and even then, it cost him his life. He did not live to see his work...his master's work...performed."

"Perhaps," I suggested, casually, "the egregore would have done better to attach itself to you. Perhaps it may yet contrive to do so. Perhaps, with your help, it might yet overcome its millennial handicap of stupidity."

"Perhaps," Dupin agreed. "And perhaps, with the help of Chopin, Battanchon and Mademoiselle Falcon, it can gather in an entire harvest of capable minds along with mine—but that has yet to be tested, and this afternoon, albeit with lesser instruments at its disposal, it could not even conquer Signor Mazzoli's, or Saint-Germain's. It has tried to capture yours before, has it not, Signor Mazzoli? And you did not need a howdah gun to withstand it then, did you?"

"No," said Mazzoli, grimly. "But it took my brother, and the woman I loved, and sent Pezza to the gallows. Nor am I convinced that it does not have all three of them still, regardless of the fact that Michele and Grigoryi are dead. Even if you are right about its lack of intelligence, there is still the matter of its power to contend with—and your friend is right. If tonight's performance goes as planned, it might make up for its long-standing lack of intelligence at a single stroke, and become infinitely more dangerous than it has been these last two thousand years."

"That is a danger," Dupin admitted, dutifully. "There is progress in all time-bound things, even ancient evil...if the *egregoroi* can be characterized as evil, given that they are by no means *purely* destructive."

Evidently, my arguments had had more effect than he had been willing to concede at the time. I closed my eyes in order that I might bathe my face in the fulgurant sunlight, still savoring the breath of wind created by the trotting horses. We were still heading southwards, although we had already past two junctions that had given the coachman opportunities to turn left, in the direction of Dupotet's residence.

"Michele never believed that he was dealing with an actual Devil," Mazzoli observed, "and nor did the rest of us, with the possible exception of Grigoryi...but we didn't know, or understand. The hill-folk, for all their crudity and ignorance, did have an inkling. They knew that the Devil in question was real, even if it was not a literal fallen angel, and that a pact sealed with clever music would have its effect, however treacherous. You've seen what the monster has done to Maddalena—it's evil, believe me."

"A Devil is what the Church called it," Dupin reminded him.

"In the sight of a jealous God, *egregoroi* could not be other than demonic—but we are rationalists now, and we know full well that everything that exists is merely natural. The *egregoroi* are not evil, in the silly sense intended by the Church, nor are they even chaotic, in the sense of being extensions or instruments of Nyarlathotep. That they are direly dangerous, I will grant, for they are predatory by nature, and feed on the stuff of souls as well as flesh...but if tigers fed on intelligence as well as flesh, would they still be mere tigers? *Could* they still be mere tigers? With consciousness comes conscience, and when silliness is finally set aside...."

"And yet," I pointed out, "even a great rationalist like yourself is a predator by nature. You eat meat, do you not, Dupin? Are you certain that if you were also required by your organism to feed on more rarefied kinds of meat, you would be any more scrupulous in your dealings with its suppliers?"

"A fair point," Dupin admitted. "And food for thought." He did not smile at his joke.

"And it has not concluded its dealings with the siren, as yet," I said. "Whether or not anything can be made of Grigoryi's dead flesh, Maddalena might yet experience a new infusion of youth."

Mazzoli's eyes had relaxed from their earlier wideness, but now they actually narrowed. "Do you think so?" he asked.

"Does it matter?" Dupin put in.

"It might," Saint-Germain observed, perhaps mischievously, "if they could both be young again."

"No!" said Mazzoli. "No yielding to temptation! I intend to destroy the cello. That will not destroy the monster, I know—but it will wreck the work it has done since Michele sealed that wretched pact, and force it to begin its wicked campaign afresh."

"It might be too late for that," Dupin said, softly. "And even if it were not, the...monster...might be harder to destroy than you imagine. Tell me—did you know what was in the box that your brother and Maddalena kept alongside the cello?"

"What box?" Mazzoli asked, his evident ignorance answering

the question.

"It contained a severed hand. Do you know whose hand it might have been, or what its significance might be?"

"Michele Pezza's?" Mazzoli asked, although his tone made it obvious that it was a wild guess.

"I doubt it," Dupin replied.

"Cagliostro's?" I suggested.

Dupin looked at me sharply. "Do you have a reason for that suggestion?" he demanded.

"No," I admitted. "It's probably a silly one. I withdraw it."

Dupin's gaze was still boring into me, and I suddenly felt uncomfortable. The carriage jolted as it made a belated left turn, and flung me forward, so sharply that Saint-Germain rose to his feet to catch me and steady me.

By the time I had recovered from the confusion and taken my seat again, Dupin had turned his head to look at Saint-Germain.

"Have you examined the hand, Monsieur le Comte?" he asked.

"Yes," said Saint-Germain. "So far as I can judge, it's not very old—not old enough to be Cagliostro's at any rate, and probably not Michele Pezza's either. All I can say for sure is that it's a man's hand, and must have been disabled even before it was severed, for the joints were so badly gnarled that the fingers could not have flexed."

I did not raise the objection that the fingers had flexed well enough when the hand had gripped mine. I had already convinced myself, for safety's sake, that I had imagined that.

"I see," Dupin said—although he did not take the trouble to explain what he had seen, if it were any more than a mere figure of speech.

"Whose hand do *you* think it was, Dupin?" I asked, although I knew that it would be futile.

"I don't know," Dupin replied, scrupulously. "I would need to examine it carefully myself before I dared to hazard a guess."

I suspected that he *had* guessed, but I knew how reluctant he was to reveal his guesses when they were based on intuition rather than evidence.

"That's easily done," said Saint-Germain, "for I...." He stopped short.

He was about to say "I have it here"—but he had realised, as he reached inside his jacket, that he did *not* have it there. For a moment, his brow furrowed as he tried to remember whether he had taken it out while he was still at home, perhaps to avoid spoiling the line of his jacket...but he had not. He had put the hand into his pocket, not wanting to leave it lying around, and somehow, between his dressing room and the cushion on which he was now sitting, it had *slipped out*. He looked on the floor of the carriage, and then stood up to inspect his seat.

The hand was nowhere to be seen. It had disappeared...as if by magic.

Dupin was about to question the Mesmerist as to what might have happened to the hand, but he had no time. The carriage stopped, and the coachman got down, in order to stick his head through the *portière*.

"I came the long way around, milord, as you asked," he said, "and kept to a moderate pace—but we're here, and by no means too early. The party seems to be in full swing already."

Saint-Germain checked his watch, and Dupin did likewise. I can only assume that they showed the same time. I did not bother to check my own. I already knew what time it was.

The sun was very low now; the western sky was purple around the bloated orb. We took our time getting down from the carriage, and paused to savor the declining day. Paolo Mazzoli left his gun behind in the carriage, without raising any argument—but I saw his eyes running along the hedge surrounding the property outside which we had stopped, and I knew that he was inquiring for weaknesses, his lust for vengeance undiminished. There were men stationed at the various doorways, who had to be policemen in spite of their livery, but I did not suppose for a moment that Paolo would be intimidated by their presence. He was an adept, after all. He was confident that, once the music began, he would be able to slip in and out unchallenged.

The twilight would be lingering, and it would be some time before the darkness was complete, but the lanterns hung by the hundred in the Baron du Potet de Sennevoy's extensive garden were already lit, casting velvety shadows by the thousand, which would gradually turn black.

It was a beautiful night for a siren song.

It was a beautiful night to create, and to feed…and perhaps to change the world. How could I tell what might and might not be possible, in a new world?

CHAPTER TWELVE
THE BARON DU POTET'S SOIRÉE

The Baron's butler was almost as impressive in his English stiffness as Saint-Germain's. When he announced our names at the entrance to the packed drawing-room, the Baron immediately hurried over to meet us. He had obviously been doing a great deal of hurrying recently. If he really had delayed sending Saint-Germain's introduction in the hope that Saint-Germain would be unable to accept it, he gave no sign of it, and greeted the Comte like an old friend.

"I'm very sorry, Baron," the President of the Harmonic Society said, unctuously. "It's terribly presumptuous of me to have brought guests—and so many of them!—but this gentleman is Signor Paolo Mazzoli, the brother of the late Grigoryi Mazzoli, known to you as Tommaso Angelotti. It is, I believe, Tommaso's composition that your august trio will be performing this evening?"

"Why, yes!" said Dupotet. "I did not realize that Tommaso had given you forewarning—he swore me to the utmost secrecy, and forbade me to send out the invitations until the last minute... an instruction I respected in spite of his untimely demise. Nor did I know that he had a brother." He paused to bow to Mazzoli before turning to Dupin. "Monsieur Dupin," he said. "I'm glad to see you—I would have sent you an invitation had I not known that you rarely attend such events." Then he turned to me and said: "I know that we've met but I'm afraid that I've forgotten your name."

"No matter," I murmured, politely. "I've all but forgotten it myself."

Mercifully, Dupotet had already turned back to his fellow *poseur*. "There's no need to apologize for bringing guests," he said. "As you can see, there's hardly anyone in the crowd who has not—and I've never known so many people to arrive so early at a *soirée*, even out of season. Knowledge of Monsieur Chopin's illness had convinced many people that he would never play again, so there is some sense that tonight's performance might be his swan song. He has agreed to play one of his own nocturnes after finishing Tommaso's, if he feels well enough."

"How is Mademoiselle Falcon's voice?" I asked.

Dupotet looked at me quizzically, evidently still annoyed with himself for not knowing who I was. "Much better, I'm assured," he said. "She has been forced to take a long rest, but she is convinced that she is ready once again to perform—she regards tonight as a trial run, not having wished to risk an appearance on the stage of the Opéra until she is quite certain that she can withstand the rigors of wholehearted effort." Again he turned back to Saint-Germain. "The doors to the garden are open, as you see," he said. "I sent out a hundred invitations, expecting fifty to provoke no response, and the remainder to conjure up an audience of eighty or a hundred, but more than three hundred people have already arrived, and I would not be surprised if we were eventually to reach four hundred. Tommaso would be very proud—it's a tragedy that he could not be here. Hopefully, tonight will be a fitting memorial for him. There's hardly anyone here who knew him, alas—he was so badly crippled by his arthritis—but in his youth he knew a great many famous people, in Paris and in Italy, including Guadagnini, Cagliostro, Puységur...."

"Fouché," I added, inaudibly.

"Is Maddalena here?" Mazzoli cut in, almost rudely.

Dupotet blinked. "Tommaso's housekeeper?" he queried. "Why, no. I met her on numerous occasions, of course, when she brought notes from Tommaso—brief notes, alas, as he could hardly hold a pen—but she's deaf, you know…she couldn't possibly…." He trailed off, uncomfortably aware of the fact that it would never have occurred to him to invite Tommaso Angelotti's housekeeper to the composer's "memorial", even if she had had the keenest hearing in the world. Fortunately, the butler announced another party of guests, and he had to hurry off at top speed to greet them.

"Quite a crowd," Saint-Germain observed, as we made our way through the open double door into the garden. "Mostly physicians, lawyers, petty administrators and clergymen, of course—that's why they're all so early, and why there's such an acute shortage of pretty wives and daughters. The *haut ton* is conspicuous by its absence, but artistic Paris is out in force. I can see Liszt…Rossini…Delacroix…and Berlioz, over there…. That's Victor Hugo—did you know that his father was the general who had Pezza hanged?—in company with Dumas and Scribe! And the Bohemians are represented too, by Banville at least. There's Leconte de Lisle, with his clique, and Gautier in his red waistcoat…and your namesake, Dupin…."

"What namesake?" Dupin asked, blinking as he turned around, having just nodded discreetly to Lucien Groix, the Prefect of Police. It was possible that he actually did not know what Saint-Germain meant.

"He's referring to George Sand," I said, leaning closer to him in order to whisper. "Her real name is Aurora Dupin, although she became the Baroness Dudevant by marriage and is nowadays known mainly by her pseudonym. She's descended from the Comtes de Saxe—another branch of your family, I assume. She's been Chopin's mistress and protector for years, although their relationship is rumored to have soured lately…not enough, apparently to keep her away tonight. Saint-Germain is right— this is a very remarkable assembly…but no more than Chopin deserves, if this really is to be his swan song. Do you suppose that Paris has ever seen such an assembly of genius before, in the month of August? In the season, perhaps, but in *August*?"

Darkness had descended now, but the lamplight still seemed soft. The heat of the day had become indolent, but had not dissipated. We strolled on through the busy garden, and then around its perimeter, the four of us remaining in a group, never pausing to speak to members of the other groups assembled there. In truth, there was little opportunity for that; although Saint-Germain recognized at least half a dozen members of the Inner Circle of his Society, the Society's rules of secrecy forbade them to hail him, and there were few other people there who knew him well enough to introduce him to their friends. The artistic luminaries he had identified by sight were not in a position to pay him the same compliment. I, alas, was in a similar situation—but I was content with that, for the time being.

The sky filled up with stars, tiny and tremulous.

"You don't seem quite yourself, my friend," Dupin observed, speaking as confidentially as I had when I had explained the mysteries of George Sand. "You seem strangely loquacious, at least in short bursts, and oddly distracted when you fall silent."

"Do I?" I said. "I hope I don't seem silly. After all, I'm not a cretin, a moron or an idiot, am I?"

There was a very audible intake of breath then, from Paolo Mazzoli, who had just caught sight of the performers setting up their instruments in the drawing-room. The grand piano was, of course, *in situ* already, and its position determined the site of the performance. There were too many people in the crowd to assemble within the room, but the piano was opposite the open doors, and the recital would be clearly audible in the garden, in spite of the competing rumor of the city and the reduction in acoustic quality that would be caused by the absence of a ceiling.

I followed the direction of Mazzoli's gaze. He was looking at Félix Battanchon, who was removing a cello from an instrument-case: his own cello, which he doubtless played night after night at the Opéra. Everyone else, I suspected, would be looking at Chopin, who seemed rather pale but not conspicuously weak. Personally, I studied Cornélie Falcon's features, which seemed a little flushed with excitement and anxiety. She was not a beautiful woman, although she was handsome enough, in a statuesque sort of way, and certainly far more imposing than Aurora Dupin.

"Where's the Guadagnini?" Paolo Mazzoli hissed, as our view of the performers was eclipsed by a general movement of the crowd toward the drawing-room—or, at least, toward the wide-open doorway looking into the drawing-room. "This isn't right...this isn't right at all."

"Is it possible that we were mistaken about Maddalena's intentions?" Saint-Germain asked, uncertainly. "We have been assuming a great deal...."

"We were right about the authorship of the composition," Dupin muttered. "But it might be the case that the Guagagnini is not crucial, by comparison with the music itself."

"Nonsense!" said Mazzoli, sharply. "You weren't there when the pact was made—I was. You didn't hear the accursed instrument play, to seal and celebrate the rite. The Guadagnini is crucial—I can assure you of that. But where is it, and where's Maddalena?"

The members of the crowd were still jockeying for position within and without the doorway, blocking our view completely. Mazzoli's eyes began to search the garden ardently, seemingly expecting to find the old woman lurking in the bushes, with the instrument-case beside her—but the garden was too large and too well-equipped with carefully-pruned bushes, tastefully organized to create nooks and arbors: the *salles de verdure* that the French love to create. If Maddalena had been able to get past the policemen guarding the doorways in the enclosing wall, there were plenty of places where she might hide, if not with a whole orchestra, at least with a string quartet.

"More complication," Dupin murmured. "Nothing in this is simple—but that, I think, is the nature of *egregoroi*, just as disorder is the nature of the chaos-spawn. That, after all, is how an egregore operates: by tangling human minds together with metaphorical strings and knots. An ordinary vampire is a simple thing—lust transfigured—but lust is a mere subsidiary lure to an egregore, which delegates its exercise to a siren, while it lays out other, subtler temptations…love of country, love of self… and above all, *love of music*. It *needs* complication…perhaps it *is* complication, in some peculiar abstract sense, some strange offspring of the forces that bind the universes together, defining the differences in their material form and spiritual animation…."

"Food for thought," I murmured in my turn. "Food for thought, indeed…but let's try not to be distracted from the task in hand."

Dupin took me by the arm then, and drew me aside, away from Saint-Germain and Paolo Mazzoli, and into the dark shadow of a linden-tree.

"Can you help it?" he asked.

"Help what?" I asked, uncomprehendingly.

"Can you help being distracted, if complication is indeed part and parcel of your nature, your essence? Can you help dividing your attention as you divide yourself?"

"What on earth are you talking about, Dupin?" I asked.

"I'm talking about the egregore," he said. "The egregore that possessed you this morning, in the catacombs, and is now using you as an instrument, just as it is using Maddalena and Dupotet…and presumably hopes to use a hundred more individuals before the night is out…perhaps leaving hundreds more sucked dry—dead, dispirited, or merely dulled to the point of common unintelligence and lack of inspiration."

"Don't be ridiculous, Dupin—it's me! You know full well that it's me!"

"I do," he said, "or else I'd almost be tempted to borrow Mazzoli's ridiculous firearm. It *is* you…but that doesn't alter the fact that you're not entirely yourself. I don't know how you feel, inside—perhaps little different from the way you felt yesterday and the day before—and I'm perfectly prepared to believe that you aren't yet consciously aware of what has happened to you… but *think about it*, my friend. Does not your own behavior strike you as odd? *How did you contrive to open that box to release the hand?*"

It pained me to think that he might be jealous of the fact that, for once, I had solved a puzzle and he had not—but what else could I think? What else could I possibly think?

"This is unworthy of you, Dupin," I said. "You're a rational man, and should not let your imagination run away with you."

"Listen to me, my friend," he said, gripping my arm urgently and insistently. "You must listen to me. You do not know what you are doing. You are following an instinct, in a fashion blurred by thousands of years of misconception and false belief. You must *think* about what you are doing. When the musicians begin to play, I suppose that you will have the upper hand—I shall be powerless to stop you, I suspect, and so will that poor fool Mazzoli. He and I, like Saint-Germain, will probably need all our reserves of courage and resilience simply to remain unpossessed...but you *must not be silly.* Please, my friend—you have a good mind, if only you will condescend to use it. If your nature really is complicated, then embrace complication, and complicate yourself further...there is so much more to the life of the intellect, and the life of the soul, than you have so far glimpsed, even in three thousand years. Listen to your own music, my friend. Listen to your own heart...and think! Above all, *think!*"

"Sometimes, Dupin," I told him, earnestly, "you seem to fall for your own line of patter, and mistake the wildest ravings of your imagination for ratiocination. Calm down, my friend, and take your own advice. Listen to the music...and your heart's response to it. Only listen...and you might find something finer by far than cold, calculating and callous thought...."

I did not have to say any more, because that was when Frédéric Chopin's distant fingers began to caress the piano, and Félix Battanchon drew his bow across the strings of his favourite cello...and Cornélie Falcon opened her mouth to give voice to the siren within...and reality began to dissolve—not to fracture, thus to let the dimensions of chaos intrude, but to soften and melt, and become a dream-dimension in itself, at least

within the confines of the Baron Du Potet's house and garden…
where the fugitive residue of the Parisian *monde* had assembled
in the oppressive but silken warmth of an August evening….

The music was beautiful. It bore no resemblance to the crazed
tarantella that Maddalena had conjured from her violin that
morning, which had been brutal and unpolished. This too was
inspired by darkness; this too was a nocturne—but darkness
is amenable to many different moods, many different dreams,
many different emotions. Some nocturnes are beautiful…and
captivating. This one, crucially, was being played on magnifi-
cent instruments, by performers of genius.

I had looked forward to that moment for such a long time. I
had never heard anything like it before.

I felt strength and vigor flowing smoothly into my limbs and
my heart…or perhaps into Chopin's limbs and heart, for there
is a vital sense in which the shared experience of music can
create a communion of mind and feeling, an empathy that tran-
scends the artificial boundaries of fugitive consciousness and
the walled self.

I knew that Chopin was drawing strength from his playing,
just as Mademoiselle Falcon was drawing strength from her
singing? What was its source? What did it matter? Was it a kind
of vampirism—a matter of drawing vital energy from others?
What if it were? Was there a single member of that audience
who would not gladly have donated a tiny fraction of his vitality
to shore up poor Chopin's weakening body, or poor Cornélie
Falcon's overtaxed voice? Were not the notes they were hearing,
and the impressions conjured up by those notes, more valuable to them by far than an infinitesimal fraction of their own
wasteful futile vigor? Is not genius generous? Does it begrudge
the contribution it makes to general wellbeing in the ordinary
intercourse of arts and minds? Is it not willing to suffer for its
creativity, even to the point of self-harm? What did it matter that
there was an egregore abroad that evening, to complicate the
perfectly natural human process by which music united hearts
and minds, and brought people together?

Auguste Dupin did not understand, and had extrapolated his misunderstanding to the extent of a mistrust of music, an instinctive repulsion—even though he had heard the harmonies of Hell himself, and played them, even as he fought them. He would not be playing any instrument tonight, though, and if he fought the music, it would be a lonely battle, for his own self-defense.

His namesake did understand, and I only had to glance in her direction to see that she was not defending herself at all. Aurora, not the Auguste with whom she shared a surname, was typical of human being. She was named for the dawn, not pomposity. She knew how to set intellect aside, when the right moment came, and give herself over to feeling. I only had to look around to reassure myself that there could be no Orpheus here, and no Odysseus either. Liszt, Berlioz, Hugo, Gautier…they were Romantics all; they loved the music. They had no thought of resisting its effects…and why should they, when they would be so carefully protected, so carefully strengthened. Why should they, when they were *en route* to paradise? Why should they, when others would be sacrificed in droves for their benefit…for the benefit of Art. They were my naturally allies; soon, I would have them all in the palm of my hand…or, to be strictly accurate, Grigoryi Mazzoli's hand.

He had had two when he was laid out in the Morgue, but one of them was not original, He had cut off his left hand twenty years before, despairing of his arthritis, and hoping that a new one might serve him better…or, to be strictly accurate, the egregore had forced him to cut it off, in the forlorn hope that the battle against his sickness could be won that way. Alas, cutting off a hand that offends you does not always solve the problem. Perhaps it never does, but one has to try…one cannot give in to the corrosions of *jettatura*, even when one sees it reflected every day in the dark eyes of one's only companion, one's only confidante.

If his brother only knew what agonies Grigoryi had gone through, in consequence of his own corrosive guilt, in the course of the last forty years…and Maddalena too. If Paolo had only known that, his eyes would have filled with tears…and perhaps he would have blown his own silly head off with his silly howdah gun….

Perhaps….

But the music was unfolding still, smoothly and harmoniously, reflecting and inspiring the August night, in all its velvet splendor and languid comfort. The sky was clear, and the stars were shining brightly now, while the silver moon, three-quarters full, was glorious in its cratered clarity. The music fitted the mood of the month, as it invaded the minds of its listeners, who felt lassitude invading their limbs as Chopin grew in strength, casting off the effects of his sickness…as Maddalena grew in strength, casting off the effects of hers…and as I grew in strength, casting off my own…for I too was sick, and had been for a very long time, entangled and eroded by my own complication, my own displacement….

Dupin, I suppose, might have said that I did not really belong in this world…in *his* world…but what gave him the authority to say that? Had I any other? Did I not have the right to feed on the nourishment I needed, not merely to sustain me but to shape me, to give me solace and pleasure, ambition and hope… and love.

Yes, love…albeit not the kind of love that either Dupin would ever recognize, or condone.

Am I truly a monster? I thought.

No, I answered. *Not a monster but a marvel—who might be welcomed by humankind, if they would only admit the true desire of their craven hearts…the desire* not to be alone.

People had died, to be sure—but what sort of people? Brutes, who had nothing to them but their crude vigor. Others had been threatened with death—but did the world really need the likes of Paolo Mazzoli? More would die, for certain—but who would miss them? Petty administrators, crooked lawyers, charlatan physicians, policemen in disguise…what did such dross matter, if some fraction of their vitality could be transferred to Frédéric

Chopin, Cornélie Falcon, Victor Hugo and Hector Berlioz? If even the most infinitesimal fraction of what was lost could be transmuted into beautiful music, to point the way to Infinity and Paradise...what price would not be worth paying? And if by far the greater fraction of that stolen force had to be invested in the egregore that was the product and the quintessence of the meeting of so many minds, was it not a just and honest fee? What monstrousness is there in bringing human beings together, in *collecting* them and *composing* them, in binding and reconfiguring them into something greater than themselves? That is not *ancient evil*; it is Art. Therre is nothing in the universe less silly.

And what heroism there sometimes is in the struggle to achieve that end! Heroic struggle not merely against the occasional opposition of the stubborn human will, but against the relentless corrosions of disease and death, which leach away an infinitely greater quantity of vital force than all the egregoroi in the world!

I had never heard the music before, because it had never existed before, but I knew it very well, having taken so long to calculate, devise and arrange it, in all its awesome complexity, with all the benefit I could obtain from modern musical theory and notation. I knew it for what it was: a maker of *nephilim*. Was it really so ridiculous to translate that word as "giants," given the magnitude of the being it might create, and the titanic scope of it potential musicality? How does musical genius come about, save—like every other kind of genius—by its possessors standing on the metaphorical shoulders of giants?

Even Churchmen conceded that it must have been fallen angels who taught humankind the arts and sciences of cooking, pottery, metallurgy, weaponry...and music. It must have been angels, whose descent might not have been a fall at all, but merely an ambitious glide, who had taught human beings the joys and benefits of *complication*, and of *possession*.

No, there was nothing monstrous going on as that magical music extended its delirium: something intricate, yes, delicate, subtle and complex...but something, in the final analysis, that might and ought to lead to a better world, a better humankind.... not in a single night, of course, nor in a single century, but one day. Of all the virtues, patience, not charity, is the greatest.

I knew that Battanchon was building up to the first *glissando*, preparing to contrive the first gentle and controlled disturbance of the texture and fabric of the world. Afterwards, he would fall asleep—but it would not matter, because the remainder of the nocturne was designed to be played by instruments that were not positioned close to one another, but widely separate, one within the house and one without, one enclosed within walls and a ceiling, and one hidden by verdure, naked to the sky. As for the singing, that was designed to become a duet. That was not strictly necessary, of course; perhaps it was a superfluous complication. But Voltaire was surely right when he judged the superfluous to be a very necessary thing, most of all in music.

I stepped rapidly into the shadows, taking Grigoryi Mazzoli's severed hand from my pocket as I did so. I had no training in the fingering of a cello, but the hand had—and now that the body to which it had once belonged was dead, its arthritis could no longer prevent it from doing its work. Dupin had, of course, been correct in saying that the hand could do nothing constructive without the tendons and muscles of a wrist and an arm—but Dupin knew little or nothing about the physics and aesthetics of possession.

Maddalena was waiting in the near-darkness of the arbor, with the stool in position and the cello already out of its case. The hand and I took up our positions, and I nestled the instrument between my thighs, lovingly. Maddalena handed me the bow and I looked into her eyes, as if into a mirror. She really was a remarkably ugly old woman, and the sight of her almost made me shudder—but her appearance was her own fault, the consequence of her own gnawing guilt. She really had loved Paolo, and human love is a stubbornly paradoxical thing, especially when spurned or subverted. Absence really can make the foolish human heart grow fonder...but I really thought that she and I might put an end to that sort of foolishness, with a touch of genius and the right assistance.

"Soon," I whispered, "you shall be young again. Soon, you will be a siren again, with a voice that no one can resist. Soon, if all goes well, we shall have this New City at our feet, metaphorically speaking, and you shall be a queen of sorts...while I shall be greater by far than any mere king. The summer of the *egregoroi* is here at last, and we are its first humble witnesses...."

That was the moment at which Félix Battachon played the first *glissando*, and the cognitive roots of the human world shifted and stirred, and the possibility of human perception altered...momentarily, for now.

CHAPTER THIRTEEN
THE SECOND GLISSANDO

A *glissando* really is a remarkable thing. The one that Battanchon executed to perfection did exactly what Dupin had said that it would, achieving a *radical harmonic destabilization* in the mind of everyone who heard it, and hence in the possibility of their perception. Whether matter itself was reconfigured, I could not tell, but the seamless change of pitch, so challenging and so promising, certainly turned sensation topsy-turvy, and wrought a complete alteration of faculty that consciousness possessed to collect and compose sensation.

Even before that moment, I had been aware, if only peripherally, of being both myself—my *old* self—and the egregore. I had known that I was *possessed*, and had been possessed since I had heard the warped, pathetic glissando in the catacombs, so weak in its effect that any mere gypsy fiddler might have contrived it had his fingers been clever enough. It was not until I heard Battanchon's glissando, however—played on a first-rate instrument with expert fingers—that I became fully conscious of my possession, and my self-possession.

I became conscious then not merely of my old self but a veritable host of others: of poor Michele Pezza, whose generalship had always been inadequate against the might of France; of Cagliostro, who had turned out to be such a weak reed; of Maddalena, the siren spoiled by grief; of Grigoryi Mazzoli, the would-be immortal who had been barely able to resist the acid of self-loathing; of a thousand others to whom I could not even put names, all of them dull and complicated and beset by paradoxes of desire and imagination. There was no need for them to walk abroad as intangible ghosts or cold-fleshed vampires; they were all within me now, warm and safe, as familiar as faces in a mirror, and in no way offensively supernatural, or even insultingly extraordinary...save only for their unusual number, their inextricable complication.

Dupin had been right about that, I supposed. The very essence of an egregore is complication, for the essence of an egregore is multiplication, and there is more complication than enough even in a single possessed mind, let alone a multitude. The independence of an egregore, by comparison with any merely individual vampire, is its strength, but also its weakness. That which has no definite and permanent location is hard to kill, but that which has no definite and permanent location also finds it direly hard to *act*...especially when it is forced by unkind circumstance to seek containment in diseased flesh and inanimate objects. From such a base, inspiration is not so very difficult, but *action*—the deployment of physical force, upon solid matter, which is often recalcitrant even when it has no guiding intellect—is a very different matter.

I was holding Grigoryi Mazzoli's severed hand in my own right hand, but as Battanchon's glissando reached its terminus, I transferred it to my left. This time, it did not grip mine in a sinister handshake, but fused with it instead. Whether Grigoryi's hand melted into mine, or mine into Grigoryi's, it is hard to say—but where there had been two hands, one dead and one alive, there was now one, both dead and alive.

Naturally—if I dare to use such a silly word in such an exotic context—the effect of the fusion went beyond mere fingers. Out of all the shades populating my possession, Grigoryi Mazzoli now stood out, brightened by consciousness. We were already fused, already one, but it was not until I adopted his hand that I really understood the nature and extent of his own self-hatred.

With consciousness comes conscience, but people sometimes forget that when they make their plans; they anticipate the material outcomes of their actions, but not the penalties they might exact of themselves in consequence. It had been one thing for Grigoryi to plan the betrayal of Michele Pezza, his friend and leader, and Paolo, his loving brother, and Maddalena, whom he considered to be a mere peasant, a mere instrument, a mere siren, but was, for all of that, a human like any other, with dreams and emotions and ambitions of her own...but it was another for him to look back on what he had done, and know himself. Had he been an evil man, or merely an unfeeling man, things might have been different, but....

Complications, and more complications.

It is not easy to be called a monster, even when one has the means to deny one's monstrousness. When one calls oneself a monster....

It is not easy to be a parasite on human thought and feeling, as well as human flesh, and it becomes direly difficult when thought, feeling and flesh turn against one another and themselves....which they do, all too often. People disappoint themselves, as well as one another.

The best thing of all, it is said, is not to be born, and after that to die young...but no entity that becomes conscious of that fact can ever achieve that paradoxical ambition. Perhaps the next best thing is to be a lump of wood or a tapeworm...but that too is out of reach. Cursed with consciousness, we are all doomed—are we not?—humans and superhumans alike, to seek solace in something, be it intellect, or sensual indulgence...or music?

Perhaps, if one cannot surrender existence, or consciousness, the best of all *possible* worlds is....

Battanchon's instrument fell silent then, and the final reverberations of the world-dissolving glissando died away. I began to play. There was no division within myself, no sense in which I was merely plying the bow, while poor dead Grigoryi, his flesh reduced to a borrowed hand, gripped the neck of the instrument like some strange hunting-spider, picking out the notes with his fingers.

I played, and I was whole, and self-possessed.

It *was* complicated, and irritatingly so—but if magic were simple, and easy, the world would have fallen into chaos long ago.

The way has to be prepared, and carefully; the greatest virtue of all is patience. Music has a logic of its own, and cannot be hurried, either in is composition or its performance. A crescendo has to be built...and I set out to build it, with Frédéric Chopin's virile collaboration, and Cornélie Falcon's wondrous dark soprano voice to complete the spell.

I was happy—happier, I think, than I had ever been before... although memory is a fickle sieve, and I knew full well that I had forgotten far more of my long existence than any memory could ever have retained...but I felt safe, and confident, buoyed up by the music, by Chopin's genius, and Mademoiselle Falcon's siren song, and my own virtue and virtuosity. I gave my collaborators strength, as I took strength from elsewhere. I created them as they created me. And every single member of that audience had cause to be grateful to me; every single member of that highly select, multi-talented, utterly modern audience had cause to love me, to thank me...even those who might die in an ecstasy of bliss, as the substance of their souls was redistributed.

No one had any cause for complaint, morally or emotionally.

I watched Maddalena grow younger. I watched her grow more beautiful. I gave her everything she had lost, and more. I watched her features flow, even though the lantern-light that reached the arbor where we stood was feeble and the starlight was occluded by the branches of the linden-tree. I watched her with my human eyes, even as I felt her transformation from within her own once-treacherous flesh.

I gave her beauty. I gave her ecstasy. What more could she want? I made her, once again, into a siren...my siren.....

And when she opened her mouth to sing, in harmony with her sister, the dark soprano, I had never heard anything so beautiful in all my life.

It was perfection...and nothing remained to be done, to be

imagined, to be thought…nothing remained, but the second and final glissando, which would complete the rite….

And that, as absurd as it seemed, as insane as he must have been, was when Paolo Mazzoli appeared at the entrance to the *salle de verdure*, with his stupid, idiotic, monstrous howdah gun in his hand—the most perverse malcontent imaginable. The music had actually assisted him, when he went to fetch the weapon from the waiting carriage, by lulling the policemen who might have stopped him at the doorway into a false sense of security.

He saw me—not as myself, but as his brother Grigoryi, returned from the dead.

And he saw Maddalena, as he had known her long ago: young, beautiful, bewitching.

But he pointed the gun anyway, as if to fire from the hip: the gun that was impossible to aim, but was capable of turning all or any one of us—myself, Maddalena or the Guagadgnini— into bloody shreds if fired at point-blank range.

Secret policemen should have been hurling themselves at his shoulders and knees to bring him down, but they were not; they were entranced by the music, lost within the innermost recesses of their not-so-secret selves…exactly as he should been, but was not.

"This is impossible," I said. "You resisted me once before, but I was infinitely weaker then. You cannot do this. It cannot be done."

I was wrong, obviously, but I was also right. He was no Odysseus, and certainly no Orpheus, but he had not only contrived to resist the spell of the music; he still had the power of action. He raised the gun—but he was still nearly ten meters away. Scattered, the shot would not have nearly so lethal an effect. He had to move closer in order to be certain of killing the cello—and he could not do it.

He took one step forward, but that took almost all the reserves of strength to which he was clinging so desperately. Perhaps he could have taken another, given time. Surely, though, given the time in question, I would have reached the second *glissando*, and raised a signpost to Infinity such as no one in Paris had ever experienced before.

The time was not given. Maddalena hurled herself forward, not just by one step but several—perhaps as many as a dozen. She was as firmly in my possession as she had been since Saint-Germain's symbolic hand had reclarified her mind sufficiently to allow her to become a viable object of possession again, but I was more thinly spread now, more focused in the glorious, generous music, and she was different too. She was young again, a siren again, unsimplified again. What she did, I did; we were performing in unison...but we were not in full conscious control of our actions. The music had opened a pathway into the unconscious mind...and beyond.

My lovely siren was not trying to sacrifice herself to save the violin. We could not imagine, even for a fleeting instant, that Paolo would actually be able to fire the gun at her. We were convinced that he would surrender it to her, that she would make it safe, and remove the last possible obstacle to our success. We would not even have hurt him once we had it in our possession—although he might have been diminished to the point of helplessness and idiocy in the interests of Art.

It should not have gone wrong, and there is no way to know exactly how it did. Paolo was undoubtedly confused and conflicted. He did not understand what Maddalena was doing when she ran toward him. In all probability, he no longer understood what he was doing himself. Perhaps he was trying to discharge the gun harmlessly into the air, in a desperate attempt to subvert the magic of the music without obliterating it completely...without condemning the siren Maddalena to her former voiceless plight.

Whatever the cause, or combination of causes, when we—when Maddalena—reached out to take the gun from Paolo's hands, the barrels were angled upwards, and when their loving hands made contact for the first time in more than forty years, the gun went off.

The greater part of the shot contained in the cartridge was harmlessly discharged, but the remainder hit us—hit her—and the range was, indeed, point-blank.

The gun's muzzle velocity was relatively low, and intentionally so, for the whole object of the weapon was to make sure that a close-placed target would absorb all the energy of the blast. My siren, my lovely siren, took such impact as there was full in the face, and the pellets pulverized her brain.

It was not so much a deluge of bloody shreds that peppered me as a few stray droplets of sticky rain, and most of those fell on my own face and shoulders. I had no cause to stop playing, and the Guadagnini did not pause in its work as I continued to ply the bow. Nor did Cornélie Falcon stop singing, in the distant drawing-room.

The duet of human voices became a solo, but that in itself could not spoil the magic. The detonation of the gun disturbed the nocturne, too—and that was a greater threat, but not an unmanageable.

All was not lost…but I knew that my resources would now be stretched to their ultimate limit, and that, even as my power approached its anticipated maximum, I would be at my most brittle and my most vulnerable….

The power of the human mind to disregard unwelcome interruptions is remarkable, especially when a magnetic spell has entranced an entire crowd, binding its attention into an odd kind of introspection. The members of the audience heard the detonation, but their minds—with less than handful of exceptions—did not want to register its impact. Their minds wanted to hear Frédéric Chopin's piano, Cornélie Falcon's voice, and Grigoryi Mazzoli's cello. The momentary explosion and the continued absence of Maddalena's voice were observed and ignored, blotted out of consciousness. The vast majority of the audience members only wanted to hear and belong to the music…only wanted to hear and belong to *me*…and why should they not? Who could offer them anything better?

The shot did not echo, thanks to the stifling effect of the

surrounding greenery. It did, however, leave a physical and psychological recoil for Paolo Mazzoli—poor, stupid Paolo—to absorb. The combination of the two brought him to his knees, in shock, pain and despair.

He had only fired one of the two cartridges; the second barrel had already rotated into position in front of the firing-pin. He could have fired again, perhaps to blow his own idiotic brain to smithereens, but he no longer had the strength, or the necessity. He knew what he had done, although he had not been able to anticipate its effect.

He had thought himself hardened to all temptation, all magic; he had believed that he had made himself into a mere instrument of vengeance, implacable and unstoppable. He had not reckoned with the propensity of his own heart to break, in response to a telling impact.

He dropped the gun, and collapsed for a second time, this time screwing himself up into a fetal position—not quite dead, as yet, but no longer wholly alive. His self-possession had collapsed too, and his powers of resistance with it.

Then the Comte de Saint-Germain stepped awkwardly over Paolo's inert body, and picked up the gun. He did not step over Maddalena, though; he paused, alive but sandwiched by death.

"You too?" I murmured, so softly that only he could possibly hear me. "But why not? If Paolo could withstand the music, why not you? Where's Dupin?"

"Who cares, Signor Angelotti?" said Saint-Germain. "This is between you and me now. I'm here to bargain, not to fight."

"You want a pact?" I said. "Granted." There was no time for bargaining—and in any case, I had to care about Dupin's whereabouts, for he had just made his appearance too, as if on cue, and I thought, momentarily, that I might yet need Saint-Germain to shoot him, to reduce him to ashes and dust...or at least to threaten to do so.

Dupin was unarmed—or so I thought. Dupin was harmless—or so I thought.

"I know who you are, my friend," Dupin said. "You might

resemble Grigoryi Mazzoli now, but I know who you really are."

"Shoot him," I said to Saint-Germain. "Those are my terms."

I didn't *really* need Saint-Germain to shoot Dupin—not unless he moved further forward, at any rate. I only needed to delay him, until the magical music reached the second *glissando*. The threat, I thought, would be enough for that.

Saint-Germain didn't point the gun at Dupin, though. He didn't point it at me either, but that wasn't something I feared unduly, in a creature as full of complex and paradoxical doubts as he was. He was convinced, now, that he really was the Comte de Saint-Germain, returned from the dead, and he knew that he owed that awareness to me. I couldn't possess him—yet—but I didn't have to. He wanted a pact. Self-possession is a wonderful thing, and its enhancement by magnetic talent or training is a wonder too, but he who would increase self-possession must be careful of the self he aspires to possess....

"How can I trust you?" the fake Comte asked, uneasily.

He right, of course. How could he? There was no way I could persuade him that he could, because he couldn't.

"Point the gun at the sky, Saint-Germain," Dupin said to the charlatan who had fallen victim to his own line of part. "Timing is everything now, but if you judge the moment right, you might yet disrupt the spell. The first detonation has sown unease—a second might just spoil everything, with a little luck—but you probably need to fire as soon as the concluding *glissando* begins, and you definitely need to fire before it reaches its terminus. If you miss the critical moment...."

I wasn't afraid. I didn't think Saint-Germain could do it—in himself, he was too hesitant, incapable of trust in spite of being so avid to make a diabolical pact...and he didn't like Dupin. He might not be wholly conscious of the fact himself, but he envied Dupin bitterly, and was afraid of him. When the crucial moment came, he wouldn't do what Dupin required of him, any more than he would do what he imagined that I required of him.

Dupin was powerless. Dupin had lost.

I was safe. I was there. It was settled.

I embarked upon the second, concluding *glissando*, ripping reality apart.

The howdah gun did not fire. Saint-Germain had not even pointed it at the sky. But we were not finished with impossibilities.

It was Maddalena who spoiled the second glissando: my very own siren, my most obedient slave. She had risked and lost her life for us—for me—because or in spite of everything that had been gifted to her...but she had subverted and damned me too.

Tiny fragments of her flesh had showered me, albeit lightly—including, although I had not realized it at the time, the part of me that was the Guadagnini. The bloody droplets had had no immediate perceptible effect—but the residue of one of them had made the lower reaches of the instrument's neck sticky, and when my fingers—my poor possessed fingers—attempted the second sweeping *glissando*, they were interrupted in their glide.

Perhaps the physical stickiness would have been enough to spoil the effect, and perhaps not, but the fingers that whose slide was producing the *glissando* had been borrowed by magic, and they were sensitive in a fashion that went far beyond the physical. The same was true of the stickiness itself, which was no random flesh and blood but magically-rejuvenated flesh and blood....a siren's flesh and blood....*Maddalena*'s flesh and blood.

Even dead, she was not free of my possession...but he who would increase possession must be careful of the selves he aspires to possess. Humans, like egregores, and for exactly the same reasons, are essentially untrustworthy.

My magical fingers absorbed Maddalena's flesh as they had absorbed Grigoryi's hand...or were absorbed by them...and with the same determination to play...or to improvise....

The *glissando* faltered—if that is not a ridiculous understatement. The *glissando* was *transformed*. Its smooth transition was distorted, and so was its transgressive indicator of infinity.

Reality faltered too, hesitating over its reconformation.

It was impossible, but it was also Fate.

More importantly, it was consciousness.

Had I been doing what Dupin had demanded of me, and thinking? Of course I had. How could I avoid it? Had I been thinking thoughts whose like I had never experienced before, in three thousand years? Of course I had. Was it not August 1846, in the Age of Enlightenment, Industrialization and Science? Was I not in possession of a man—a man in duplicate—who, though doubtless emotionally crippled, was far from being a fool?

Magic does not need to be perfect; even a spoiled *glissando* can take effect. My bid for power was not an all-or-nothing affair. Perhaps I could have concluded my business, in spite of the flaw in the instrument's performance—my performance— had it not been for the effect that the flaw had, on my conscious- ness and my intelligence....

Because, in that slight falseness of the climactic change of pitch, I experienced a doubt, a revelation, a *realization*.

I realized that I had underestimated the nature and extent of my potential domain. I had been confident that there was no Orpheus, no Odysseus, among my potential possessions, who might resist my siren song by means that were familiar to me... but I had not even begun to understand the kinds of resistance that might and would be mounted by a Paolo Mazzoli, a Comte de Saint-Germain, or an Auguste Dupin.

The world had already been transformed while I had been patiently taking refuge: the world of perception, thought, imagi- nation and composition, that is. I had been unready to see that, when I emerged from my refuge, let alone to admit it. I was not a cretin, a moron or an idiot, but there *was* a sense in which I had been ever so slightly silly. I had not realized that the limits of possibility had shifted, and that the supernatural really was under threat of being reduced, in the possibility of perception, to the merely natural.

If I had ever had a chance of properly gripping—of *taking possession*—of the minds of Chopin and Liszt, Mendelssohn and Delacroix, Hugo and Dumas, Gautier and George Sand, I lost it in that moment of realization. I lost it in that moment of self-doubt. I lost it in an inefficient glue that was compounded out of blood and vulgar meat…but which was not, even in that state, without identity, nor immune to the paradoxes of desire.

"Oh, Maddalena!" I whispered, as the Guadagnini fell silent, followed almost immediately by Chopin's piano and Mademoiselle Falcon's voice. "Oh, Parthenope. What wonders we might have wrought, had you not been merely human!"

But they had been all too human—and so, in spite of my evident superhumanity and miraculous ubiquity, had I.

"What happened?" Saint-Germain asked, staring down at the unfired cartridge that was still in the breech of his ugly gun.

"Almost nothing," Dupin replied. "Mercifully, almost nothing…except that we have heard a very fine piece of music, which will echo in our souls for the rest of our lives, even if we cannot quite remember how it was supposed to go."

He came to me, then, and said: "With luck, you will recover your true self, now." I had no way of knowing whether he was still seeing me as Grigoryi Mazzoli or as his friend…whose name, for the moment, I could not quite remember….

"Given time," I told him, "I think I might."

"That cello is mine," Saint-Germain stated, then—although he corrected himself quickly enough. "It is the property of the Harmonic Philosophical Society of Paris, and I demand that you hand it over, cursed or not."

"I fear that it's more than a little dirty," I said, as I acceded to his demand. "You'll have the Devil of a job getting it clean, I fear."

"And it might never be the same, even if you can," Dupin put in.

I noticed something lying at my feet, and picked it up—but I had to give that to Saint-Germain too, because that was also the legitimate property of the Harmonic Philosophical Society of Paris.

It was a severed human hand.

In order to accept it, Saint-German had to set the howdah gun down on the ground—which was perhaps as well, else he might have been thrown to the ground himself by a dozen disguised policemen.

It was Lucien Groix himself who picked up the weapon, for safe keeping. I had just enough consciousness left to see him turn to Dupin, presumably in order to demand an account of the murder that had been committed a few minutes before, and to know the identity of the murderer.

By the time Dupin replied, I had collapsed—knowing, as I did so, that I was likely to be absent for quite some time.

I had finally fallen victim to the quintessence of August.

CHAPTER FOURTEEN
HARMONY RESTORED

The first person I saw when I eventually woke up was a nurse—a hard-bitten professional hired from the Saltpêtrière rather than a soft-hearted amateur recruited from some convenient convent. The first thing I asked her was not where I was, or whether I might have a glass of water, but where Dupin was.

She told me that I was at home, in bed, and gave me a glass of water. Then she told me that Dupin had been at my beside for sixteen hours out of every twenty-four since I had been taken ill, but that he was only human, and needed sleep. I knew that he would be back, because I knew that he would be enthusiastic to observe and track my condition, and to ask me penetrating questions about my psychological condition.

The second person I saw, however, when I woke again, was Pierre Chapelain, who had been summoned in his capacity as a physician. He ausculated my chest, gave me a glass of water, instructed me to eat some beef broth, assured me that I would not die, and told me Dupin would resume his post by my bedside as soon as humanly possible. I had every confidence in his prognosis.

"That's a peculiar double wound you have in your neck," he observed. "Had I not been told that it had been inflicted by the tip of a stiletto, I could almost have believed that it was the bite of a vampire."

I touched the double scab. Evidently, the bandit in the alleyway had pricked me twice. "I shall wear the stigmata with pride," I assured him

The next person I saw by my bedside when I woke, though, was the Comte de Saint-Germain. He gave me a glass of water and told me that I would make a full recovery, but seemed rather disappointed when my only reply was to say: "Where's Dupin?"

"He'll be here soon," he assured me. "You might be a little grateful, you know. I have every admiration for American self-sufficiency, but one really cannot live in a house like this without servants, in Paris of all places. I have lent you my second cook and my most experienced valet, at least until you are back on your feet again. Keep them as long as you need them. I would gladly have served as your physician too, but Dupin insisted on consulting Chapelain instead. Even after everything that has happened, he still does not trust my art or my honesty."

"What day is it?" I asked.

He had perspicacity enough to know that I did not mean the day of the week. "The second of September," he told me. "The heat-wave has broken, and there is a tangible westerly wind, blowing in the breath of the fields...which is, I far, extensively tainted with the reek of burnt stubble. Even that seems healthy, though, by comparison with the miasma of the sewers. If it were not for the heavy responsibilities that fall to me as president of the Harmonic Society, I would probably spend the entirety of August on the Breton coast, but I'm a prisoner of duty."

In order to demonstrate his truthfulness, at least on the first point, he threw open my bedroom window. The odor of burning was faint but distinct. Given that the fields whose stubble was being burnt must be many miles away, the impression testified to both the strength of the breeze and the imperiousness of the odor.

"There must be more legacies to collect in August than any other month," I observed.

He did not smile. "Twelve people died in the wake of the Baron Du Potet's soirée," he informed me. "Seven on the premises—all heatstroke victims, it seems, save for the gypsy who was shot. We feared, briefly, that you might make thirteen."

"Not *almost nothing* after all, then," I said, contradicting Dupin's judgment. "Added to the number who had already been killed, twelve is not trivial."

"But not atypical," Saint-Germain assured me. "One stabbed, one shot and twelve put to death by heart failure, suffocation, dehydration and hallucination is a drop in the ocean by comparison with total death-toll attributable to such causes in the last few days of August in Paris. Dupin told me that himself, on the authority of the dutiful statisticians of the Prefecture and the Palais de Justice."

"The eleven, apart from Maddalena, who died during or after the soirée attracted no particular attention, then?" I queried.

"All perfectly natural, according to the official record… as your demise, too, would have been recorded, had it come to that. The draining of vital energy by an egregore is not yet recognized among the causes of death that can be listed in the Archives of State."

"Is Chopin…?" I began.

"No worse than before, if rumor can be trusted. No better, alas, and distressed by his quarrel with Dupin's namesake, but no worse. Mademoiselle Falcon will not be returning to the stage, though. That one performance was enough to overstretch her fragile voice."

"Paolo?"

"Not quite dead, but he'll never face a tribunal, and the circumstances of his crime have been carefully covered up— more, I suspect, to protect the policemen who were on hand to prevent any such occurrence than to avoid embarrassment to the Baron. Four policemen were among the dead, although they had seemed perfectly robust beforehand. One never can tell, it seems…."

"And the egregore?"

"I was hoping that you might be able to tell me. I've consulted Dupin, of course, but you know how evasive he can be when he refuses to reach a conclusion, or even to formulate a theory. Are you still possessed?"

"How can I possibly be sure?"

"You've spent far too much time in Dupin's company these last ten years. How can you not?"

"I wasn't aware of being possessed before. You doubtless observed, as Dupin did, that I wasn't quite myself, but that was more obvious to others than to me, at least until it was pointed out. It wasn't like being invaded by an alien presence; I was never aware of sharing my consciousness with something radically *other*, even when I was briefly confused with Michele Pezza, Grigoryi Mazzoli and others. I never had any moment of revelation informing me that I was no longer the person I had always believed myself to be."

"If you're trying to slight me," Saint-Germain said, without any hint of resentment, "you might as well save your breath. My revelation was not that I was not the person I believed myself to be, but that I am…that it was my doubts as to the possibility of my true identity that were needless. I really am the Comte de Saint-Germain."

"Resurrected or reincarnated?" I queried.

"You, of all people, should know that death is not necessarily an end…that life sometimes goes on, in more strange ways than one.

Should I? I wondered. *Or would I do better to insist that August heat can be a dangerous thing, and that enfevered brains can produce the most remarkable hallucinations?* What I said aloud, however, was: "Did I really play the Guadagnini?"

"Like a maestro," he assured me, "except for that final blunder—which the audience were generous enough to overlook, given that they'd come to hear Chopin, Mademoiselle Falcon and Battanchon, all of whom were flawless. You were very impressive, considering that you were improvising all the while, having no score to consult. Indeed, when I first saw you with the instrument between your knees, I was almost convinced that you were Tommaso Angelotti—or Grigoryi Mazzoli—returned from the dead and wonderfully rejuvenated, glorying in his own composition. Strange light and lingering heat in a *salle de verdure* can cause peculiar delusions…although I'm sure that you don't need me to tell you that. Not that I'm accusing you of *mere* delusion: whatever Dupin might say about *somnimusicality*, you and I both know that you were authentically, and utterly, possessed."

"Given that there was no written score for my part of the performance," I said, thoughtfully, "it's unlikely that anyone will ever be able to play that music again—unless someone can improvise my part by consulting Chopin's."

"I rather doubt that will be possible," he said, "although it seemed to me that you harmonized very well with the great man—and mine is not an uneducated ear. To the rest of the audience, the substituted cello and the second singer were merely part of the performance—a modest innovation, made half in jest—but they would certainly have noticed had your playing not blended in very well with Chopin's. You were possessed by true supernatural genius. You and I know that…and so, in his heart of hearts, does Dupin. One day, you know, I shall force a breach in his stubbornness. One way or anther, I shall persuade him that I really am an adept, and that there are more things in heaven and earth than are dreamed of in the positivist philosophy. I'm determined to bring him into the ranks of the Harmonic Society, if only to ensure that he makes us a gift of his book collection in his will."

I was about to wish him good luck in that particular hopeless quest when Dupin made his entrance—but he hastened away almost immediately to fetch me a drink of water.

"Will you fetch me some paper, quills and ink, before you go?" I asked Saint-Germain,

"Certainly," he said. "Is because you want to remember, or to forget—or merely to provide fuel for your American friend's career?"

I wasn't sure—but I knew that I ought to write, and hastily, so that I would have something concrete to jog my memory if ever I decided to compose a more elaborate version of the adventure (as, evidently, I have).

"Chapelain has assured me that you're on the mend," Dupin said, on his return, with a sly sideways glance at Saint-Germain—who merely rolled his eyes to signify that his pride as a physician was beyond injury from Dupin's preference.

"If you need anything else," the Comte told me, "send my valet with a note. Keep him as long as you need him—and the cook too. I can spare them." And with that, he went to fetch the items I had requested, before taking his leave.

"I'm sorry that I wasn't here when you woke up," Dupin said, taking the chair that Saint-Germain had vacated. "How do you feel?"

"Quite well," I assured him, "And entirely myself."

"That's good."

"According to Saint-Germain, you've judged me a victim of heat-induced hallucination, with a light spicing of somnimusicality?"

Dupin sighed. "What I actually said to him," he told me, "was that I could not be absolutely certain that there was anything more to your experience than that, for lack of solid evidence."

"But you do believe that I was possessed by an egregrore? And that I was by no means alone in being thus possessed?"

"Yes, indeed. My only difficulty is in determining exactly what that might mean."

"But Saint-Germain is wrong to declare that you have no theory—it's simply that you do not care to share your theory with him?"

Dupin sighed again. "What I actually said to him is that one should not credit mere conjectures with the rank of theory…and that my conjectures were probably worth no more than his."

"Which was false modesty," I judged.

"Perhaps. In a methodological sense, of course, all conjectures might be deemed equal until they have been tested—but I have sufficient confidence in my own wisdom, by contrast with Saint-Germain's, to imagine that my conjectures are at least more philosophically respectable than his."

I was already weary of his pedantry. "Has the egregore really gone?" I asked him, bluntly. "Am I free of it?"

"Not entirely," he replied—which was not the reply I had been hoping for. He hastened to add: "But I doubt that it will trouble you again in the same way, unless you invite it to return…and I cannot imagine that you will."

"Indeed not," I murmured—but I could not help reflecting that the entity could not have afflicted me in the first place had it not been invited by Maddalena, by Grigoryi Mazzoli, by Michele Pezza, and many others whose names I did not know. All of them had sought, one way or another, to possess its power…and all of them had ended up possessed, irredeemably and to their cost. I could not imagine that I would invite such an entity into my consciousness again, but I could imagine that someone like Saint-Germain might—and that, I realized, was why Dupin would never trust the man, no matter what peace offerings he made.

"You have had a narrow escape," Dupin said, "and I'm sorry to have exposed you to the danger, when you might have been safe on the coast or in the mountains. I know that you only stayed in Paris for my sake."

"I did help, though, didn't I?" I said. "Had I not been here, events might have taken a turn for the worst."

"That's true," he conceded, readily.

"And even if the egregore is not *entirely* gone, it has at least retreated to its lair in the dream-dimensions for a little while?"

"Perhaps—but I'm not so sure that *egregoroi* belong to the dream-dimensions rather than the realm of consciousness. If they have lairs there to which they retreat, it is not because they are native to another world than ours. That, at least, is my…conjecture. I think that they might be better reckoned as by-products of consciousness…warped and mistaken by-products, perhaps, but nevertheless at home there."

I remembered what I had said to Saint-Germain about having had no consciousness of any alien invasion when the possession took hold, or the presence of something essentially *other* while

I was under its sway.

"You'll have to explain," I told him.

That, as always, he was glad to do. I think that was my function in his life: to listen to his explanations; to save him from the loneliness of having no sympathetic ear but his own.

"I have often remarked that consciousness is no mere collector of experience, but a composer thereof," he told me. "Nor is it content with mere synthesis of sensory data. Music is not only the most obvious but the finest example we have of the ability of consciousness to compose new experience for its education and hallucination, its instruction and delight. Music is an aspect of human existence that draws us closer to the edges of that experience, not only reproducing but supplementing the effects of profound and extreme emotion. There is a kind of yearning intrinsic to consciousness that is the foundation of all ambition and all progress, the driving force of personality and history alike, and music is not only capable of expressing that yearning, perhaps more clearly than any other product of mind, but is capable of extending and reshaping it. When it does so, consciousness cannot help but conceive its own amplification as something external and transcendent, with a life of its own—nor can it help bundling it with other kinds of yearning, in various different ways.

"We have images a-plenty of supposedly-supernatural beings that parcel such commonplace yearnings as lust and cupidity, but they do not exhaust the kinds of yearning we have, for communions of mind that are not necessarily anchored in sex, or parental love, or any other kind of elementary association. The *egregoroi* are a subtler kind of force than common-or-garden vampires and succubi, and more readily associated with the purity of music than such creatures of lust, but they are not so very different in kind, and their origins must surely lie within us rather than without. It is not so very hard to see how they might be mistaken for angels instead of demons, in spite of the tax they impose on psychological well-being. They are complicated—perhaps, as I have already suggested, they are the very essence of interpsychic complication—but that is their virtue as well as their awkwardness. They destroy in the name of creativity, and perhaps that is enough for their actual and potential victims to reckon them intrinsically evil...but perhaps not entirely so, and surely not in their own estimation."

"But that kind of psychological explanation implies that the egregore really was something that I conjured up in my own mind—if not by virtue of heatstroke, by courtesy of some quirk of mistaken mentality...which is worse, in its way."

"To some extent, perhaps—but the seed had to be planted from without, by suggestion if not by any other means. The egregore really did *infect* you, as if you had breathed in a noxious miasma. It does have an identity and an existence independent of the individual minds it parasitizes—but so do ideas, beliefs, myths and all manner of other products of mind, which can be equally insidious and possessive in their way. The greatest enemy of all such subversive invaders is the power of rational thought; that is the sword with which their draconian cunning may be defeated. I'm speaking poetically now, rather than pedantically...proper understanding requires both kinds of discourse."

"And music too," I added.

"Indeed," he agreed. "I must be careful not to neglect it or shy away from music in future...although I must say that my instinct in that respect was not without its underlying reason."

"But for a sticky fragment of problematic flesh," I remarked, feeling a paradoxical pang of regret as well as a profound thankfulness, "my contrary instinct might have led me to oblivion, at the head of a *danse macabre* of callous physicians, miserly lawyers, petty administrators and self-important clerics—all to sustain a monster's delusions of grandeur and its patronage of genius."

"A humble fragment of flesh," he reminded me, earnestly, "is all that separates every one of us from oblivion. We have every reason to be grateful to those fragments, in spite of their problematic aspects."

ABOUT THE AUTHOR

Brian Stableford was born in Yorkshire in 1948. He taught at the University of Reading for several years, but is now a full-time writer. He has written many science-fiction and fantasy novels, including *The Empire of Fear*, *The Werewolves of London*, *Year Zero*, *The Curse of the Coral Bride*, *The Stones of Camelot*, and *Prelude to Eternity*. Collections of his short stories include a long series of *Tales of the Biotech Revolution*, and such idiosyncratic items as *Sheena and Other Gothic Tales* and *The Innsmouth Heritage and Other Sequels*. He has written numerous nonfiction books, including *Scientific Romance in Britain, 1890-1950*; *Glorious Perversity: The Decline and Fall of Literary Decadence*; *Science Fact and Science Fiction: An Encyclopedia*; and *The Devil's Party: A Brief History of Satanic Abuse*. He has contributed hundreds of biographical and critical articles to reference books, and has also translated numerous novels from the French language, including books by Paul Féval, Albert Robida, Maurice Renard, and J. H. Rosny the Elder.

www.ingramcontent.com/pod-product-compliance
Lightning Source LLC
Chambersburg PA
CBHW050742250626
47155CB00005B/1883